RIFT

ANGEL

STUART JAFFE

Rift Angel is a work of fiction. Names, characters, places, and incidents either are the product of the author's imagination or are used fictitiously, and any resemblance to any persons, living or dead, business establishments, events, or locales is entirely coincidental.

RIFT ANGEL

Copyright © 2018 by Stuart Jaffe
Cover art by Deranged Doctor Design

ISBN 13: 9781790438327

First Edition: December, 2018
Second Edition: October, 2019

For Gabe

Also by Stuart Jaffe

Rift

Angel

CHAPTER 1

With her head pressed against the passenger side window, Roni rapped her knuckles against the glass and imagined her fingers around the throat of her grandmother. The green hills of Ireland rolled by as Gram drove their rental car ever deeper into the heart of the country, and though a gentle rain caused the lush grass to glisten, the beauty of this foreign country could not outweigh Roni's inner fire. When it came to driving Roni crazy, Gram had never lost her touch.

"Are you going to talk to me, yet?" she asked Gram. "You barely said a word on the flight over and we've been in this car for a half-hour now. Shouldn't I know what kind of situation I'm going into? I get that you like to be in control all the time, but you're no longer the leader of this group. A little teamwork would be appreciated."

Gram, a sturdy woman in her seventies, patted the crucifix pendant resting on the shelf of her bosom. "You have got to stop being so naïve. You think you understand everything, but then you make all sorts of misjudgments based on your ignorance."

"How am I supposed to learn anything when you won't

tell me?"

The argument was too familiar, but Roni could not let it slide. Back home in Pennsylvania, things would be different. She could seek refuge at her desk in the Grand Library several secret floors below the family bookshop, *In The Bind*. She could bury her head amongst all the old journals detailing centuries of the history and events that shaped the Parallel Society. Or she could work on her favorite side-project — mapping out the endless, twisting caverns beneath the store that connected to Gram's office and housed the numerous books that were part of their sacred duty.

But this is was not Pennsylvania. This was not the Grand Library. This was Roni's first overseas trip as a member of the Parallel Society and she didn't want to blow it.

Trying to sound more like the adult she was and not the sulking teenager of long ago, Roni said, "Sully is the leader now. He ordered me on this trip, and that means that I am part of this."

"No, dear. It means that Sully believes you are ready to learn more. Not participate. Simply observe and learn."

"That's it? Don't get me wrong. I'm thrilled to be here, but if I'm just supposed to stay in the background, then what was the point of treating this like a team? He told me I'd be a big help to you. Why send us both?"

Clenching and unclenching the steering wheel, Gram said, "You have a lot to learn. Listening should be at the top of the list. Sully and Elliot and I are not going to live forever. We're old and we're tired of running the Society ourselves. When you take over, it's essential that you understand all aspects that exist regarding the work we do."

"Which is why your silent treatment is so damn infuriating."

"Watch your language."

"Sorry, but you are acting foolish. Have you learned nothing from the way you led us before? Playing everything close to the vest does not help the team work smoothly. At least give me something so I know what to be observing and learning from."

"You never change," Gram said.

Roni could not miss the bait in her grandmother's words but locked her jaw to prevent her mouth from digging deeper. She knew she was right – they had to work together — but she had to give the old woman some slack. After all, less than a year ago, Gram had been top dog in the Society. She had controlled things for so long that she must have expected to do so until her death. But Roni's involvement in the caverns with a creature called a hellspider led to a change of leadership.

She wasn't so sure Gram had forgiven her. That Sully — short, bald, with tufts of white hair ringing his head — had taken over and showed the makings of a strong leader probably irked Gram more. He was thoughtful and considerate, even if a bit reticent about taking the role away from Gram. It helped that his best friend, Elliot, always stood by his side.

The two old men had been like uncles to Roni as she grew up, and they saw her off on this trip as if sending her away to college. Elliot, smelling of campfire smoke, had pulled her into a firm hug.

Born in Kenya, raised in England, and settled in the US, he had a deep exacting way of speaking and a broad smile that brightened his dark features. "Trust Sully and trust your Gram. I know there is much you don't understand, but we need you to be on this trip."

Elliot's words echoed in Roni's head each time she felt the fire within burning hotter. Staring at the Irish hills drifting by, she swallowed back her biting comments and exhaled long and slow. "I will stand back and observe, and I will learn. If you need my help capturing this rift, you merely have to ask."

Though Gram kept her eyes forward on the road, Roni thought she caught the woman lifting her chin in triumph.

"We will not be capturing this rift," Gram said. "It's been tried before, and so far, nobody in the Society has figured out how to do it. The rift had been stabilized, for lack of better word, and every year I travel to Ireland to make sure that the system we have in place continues to operate safely."

"Wait, so, this is a maintenance check?"

"Of a sort."

Roni put her head against the glass again. "Unbelievable. I have a lot of work to do back in the Grand Library, and you all have sent me out here to watch you look at a bunch of books and say, *Yup they're still there.*"

"What do you think the Parallel Society is all about? We are keepers of a simple and pure task — to secure these accidental rifts that open between our universe and others. It is not supposed to be about excitement and daring. We try to avoid those kinds of situations from occurring. If we do our jobs right, everything is quiet and nothing is happening. It's that simple."

"You create chains and magic books that hold these universes, Elliot and his cane can heal people and open locks and I don't even know what else. And don't get me started on Sully and his golems. What's simple about that?"

Gram's mouth tightened with a knowing smirk. "You're still upset that you don't have a special power."

"No." *Maybe.* "I'm upset because you all keep asking me to prepare to lead this group in order to go on saving our world and yet you continually try to shelter me from what we have to face."

The road twisted and curved in such a haphazard manner that Roni had long ago lost her sense of direction.

Like the sudden appearance of a lighthouse on a foggy night, Gram calmed her tone and said, "Very well. Listen carefully so that you are prepared for what we're going to face."

Roni straightened in her seat and adjusted the seatbelt so she could better pay attention in comfort.

Gram continued, "There will be at least four women at the compound. Pay attention to the layout of the buildings, and be sure to observe the power dynamics between the women. It can change more often than you think. We will be escorted into an underground room where we will find the rift. If any of the set up needs to be adjusted or replaced, I will handle it. Try to avoid talking to any of the women without being rude, unless they ask you a question directly, of course. They will seem nice, kind, possibly even warm or open-minded. Don't believe it."

Gram pulled over to the side of the road where a metal gate led to a dirt road trailing off into the hills. She turned towards Roni. "I am no longer the leader of this group, but I am the leader of this mission. Once we are there, you do what I say. Do not question me in front of these women. It could be very dangerous."

"Got it. Don't trust the women. Follow your orders. Anything else?"

"Don't show me any disrespect or attitude." Before Roni could say a word, Gram raised her hand. "I'm not saying that as the person who raised you. I'm saying that because these women will pick up on your attitude towards me. If they sense any weakness, we could be in a lot of trouble."

Reading the seriousness on Gram's face, Roni nodded.

"I can do that."

"Good. Now go outside and open the gate."

Digesting all that Gram had said, Roni hurried out of the car to swing open the gate. The rusty metal whined like a bratty child. After Gram drove through, Roni closed the gate, and as she headed back to the car, she noticed a wooden sign under the protection of an alder tree.

Though weeds crept over one corner of the sign, the words could still be made out:

Croghan Abbey
County Offlay

Buckling into her seat, Roni said, "Is this a place for nuns?"

"Of a sort," Gram said as she headed up the dirt road. "They are no longer connected with the Catholic Church, though they have many of the same trappings. But don't be fooled. These women can be very dangerous. They are not to be trusted."

Driving onward, the trees thickened around them, blocking most of the daylight and cooling the air fast. It reminded Roni of the first time she stepped foot into the caverns below the bookstore — the way the temperature stayed cool no matter what the outside world was like. A chill crossed her skin.

"Got it," she said. "Don't trust the nuns."

CHAPTER 2

Roni peered into the shadowy forest as the wheels crunched the dirt and rocks below. No wonder all the old fairytales equated the forest with witchcraft and evil. Everywhere Roni looked, she saw shadows moving, lurking, watching her from the darkness. Just like discovering familiar images in the clouds, searching for horrors in the shadows proved every bit as easy.

The road broke free of the forest and led to a large, wide clearing. As they curved up a slight incline, Roni spotted a lake off to her right. To the left, a path led back into the woods. Ahead, the road opened into a large circle with a statue of the Virgin Mary in the center. With her arms held wide and open as she gazed down upon all approaching vehicles, she offered her Mona Lisa grin that both welcomed and warned all who approached.

Flower beds filled with purple butter wort and blue-eyed grass bordered the circle, and on the left, the main church rose high towards Heaven. Medieval in design, it had a bell tower up front and a long section going on out the back. To the left of the church, a colonnade walkway led to a bland, squarish building. To the right, a similar set up ended in another bland building. Off the far end of the circle, the road continued. In the distance, Roni saw a barn. Beyond that, tall corn grew in rows that stretched on as far as she could see.

The rain had ceased, and two women wearing black habits with white-trim wimples stood outside. They watched as Gram parked the car and stepped out. The older of the two women moved forward. She had a pudgy face and a stern mouth, and Roni suspected that a simple glance from her could stop a middle school classroom in its tracks.

"Lillian, it's so good to see you," the woman said.

Gram shook the woman's hand, then gestured to Roni. "This is my granddaughter, Veronica. She goes by Roni." Gram waved Roni over. "This is Sister Mary."

Roni got out of the car and shook hands with the Sister. "Pleasure to meet you."

Sister Mary gestured behind her without taking her eyes off Roni. "This is Sister Claudia. She's young enough to be my granddaughter."

Gram forced a chuckle and Sister Mary laughed harder than necessary. Sister Claudia stepped forward and shook hands with both women. She had a deceptive, gentle touch — bordering on frail.

"You'll find that everything is in order," Sister Mary said, lacing her fingers under her belly. "We take our duty very seriously."

Gram patted her crucifix. "I've never known you to do otherwise."

Both women appeared eminently pleased with each other. Gram even smiled wide enough to show her teeth — something Roni had never seen before and hoped never to see again.

Sister Claudia's eyes narrowed and with a stiff arm, she

gestured toward the church. "Perhaps we should show you the rift so you may complete your inspection and be on your way."

Sister Mary's hard glower forced Sister Claudia to lower her head and step back. "I apologize," Sister Mary said to Gram. "This one is under my tutelage. She will be taking over running the Abbey when I am no longer able. As you can see, she still has much to learn."

Gram tilted her head toward Roni. "I have one of my own."

The two old women shared a more authentic chuckle before Sister Mary led the way inside.

The narthex of the church consisted of a wide, flat stone flooring, highly polished wood trim around white plaster walls, and two heavy, rounded doors made of wood with black iron straps. On either side of the doors, statues of Jesus and Mary stood. Gesturing toward the right, Sister Mary led the way to a narrow door that opened onto a narrower staircase winding clockwise downward.

Stopping at the door, Sister Mary opened her mouth and from the shape of her lips, Roni expected to hear a simple caution — *watch your step*.

But then the screams came.

Sister Mary's hand covered her mouth. "Sister Susan. Sister Rachel."

Gram leapt to the stairwell and soared downward. The two nuns flew in behind her, leaving Roni to bring up the rear. Though she had seen Gram act fast before, Roni caught a glimpse of panic on the old woman's face — a new and different kind of fear.

The screams grew louder as they descended further under the church. The narrow, spiraling staircase made each footfall dangerous. Roni felt like a bug swirling down the drain, and she let out a held breath when they finally reached the bottom.

Though not as deep as the full length of the church, the cellar stretched far enough to accommodate a small gathering. Several feet ahead, Roni witnessed the rift flickering light in all directions — a swirling cylinder of red and orange like a fiery storm. The cylinder hovered about six inches off the ground and stopped just shy of the ceiling. Eight books on eight stands encircled this rift to another universe — at least, they were supposed to.

Three of the stands had been knocked over and their books strewn across the floor. Sister Susan and Sister Rachel sat nearby nursing a bleeding head wound for one and a bloody nose for the other.

Heat radiated off the rift. Air howled around them. Weaving in and out of that noise, Roni picked up on pained screams like the cries of children being tortured. Or animals. Or even the horrid shrieks of creatures unknown. The sounds shifted as if arriving on waves.

Gram stood where the gap from fallen books had been formed. She held open a book of her own. With her left foot planted behind for support, she pushed the book forward as if fighting against a heavy storm wind.

Over her shoulder, she said, "Quit gawking. Reset the books."

Roni rushed over to the nearest bookstand and set it in place. Divots on the floor made it easy to see the correct positioning. A long chain stretched from the bookstand to the spine of one book — red leather cover with gold trim. Roni reeled it in and set the book on the stand, opening it to face the rift. A warm, yellow glow emanated from the book and the roiling cylinder of energy dimmed slightly. The howling wind lessened.

Snapping her fingers at Sister Claudia, Roni said, "Are you going to help?"

Scowling, Sister Claudia uttered a soft but quick prayer before hurrying over to set up another bookstand.

Roni docked the final stand behind Gram. Having dealt with Gram's chains before, Roni found the alligator clip that secured the chain to the stand and yanked it off. Helping Gram avoid tripping on the stand, Roni guided her back until she could set the book down. With a flick of her wrist, Gram produced a new chain from the sleeve of her blouse. She secured the chain to the stand and punctured the book's spine with the other end.

Sister Claudia finished setting her book on its stand, but when she opened it a rod of energy snapped out of the cylinder like a lance and pierced the book, knocking it and Sister Claudia to the floor. Gram and Roni raced over to reset the stand while Sister Mary attended to her fellow nuns. As Roni replaced the stand in its proper position and Gram produced a fresh book, a strange, haunted noise came from the rift.

Roni looked back. Her mouth dried from being locked open. Her eyes widened.

A young girl appeared in the center of the firestorm — her hair parted in the middle and a peace sign pendant around her neck. She stared back at Roni like some burning mirror image. Only the closer Roni looked, the less she saw of her own face. Rather, she spotted a glimpse of herself from long ago — a younger version from a time before she had been born.

But then the mirror image raised its head, looking beyond Roni. The girl's chin trembled. She lifted a hand, reaching out through the cylinder, covered in swirls of orange and red. She reached for Gram.

"Mom?" the girl said.

As Roni snapped her head around to face Gram, the final book slid into place and was opened. Roni turned back to the cylinder and the girl had disappeared. The stormy cyclones within the cylinder muted in color and intensity. The horrid sounds diminished.

With her skin paling and her eyes searching the rift, Gram stood petrified like an alabaster statue. Her eyes welled, but tears did not fall. Roni had never seen such weakness in her grandmother.

The word *stroke* popped in her mind. As she scrambled through her thoughts for the symptoms of such a thing, another part of Roni warned that this would not be so simple. She took a hesitant step closer to Gram. Her grandmother's eyes snapped upon hers. Roni froze.

"Come with me," Sister Mary said in a gentle tone.

At first, Roni thought the nun spoke to her. However, the woman put her arm around Gram and the two shuffled toward the stairs.

"Wait," Roni said, but Sister Mary kept Gram moving.

Before Roni could follow, Sister Claudia stepped in her way. "We need your help here."

"That's my grandmother. I need to make sure she's okay."

"Sister Mary can take care of her just fine. But you and your grandmother came here to help with this rift. Do you want to explain to those women why we failed to finish securing things down here?"

Roni brushed by Sister Claudia and put one foot on the bottom stair. She glanced back at the cylinder of energy and the eight books surrounding it. If three of them had fallen so easily, they needed to make sure the rest were steadied, that they would remain standing. The two injured nuns needed first-aid. That left Sister Claudia and Roni to take care of things.

Thrusting her hands into her pockets and curling them into fists, Roni walked away from the stairs. Questions bombarded her mind, and Gram's warnings echoed against her conscience.

"Thank you," Sister Claudia said, coming up beside Roni.

"Not doing it for you. I'm here to take care of this job. The moment we're done, I'm taking my grandmother and leaving this place."

"I think that's a wise decision."

Sister Claudia walked over to Sister Susan and gazed at the nun's injuries. Roni did not move. Her mind, her ears, every part of her being, tried to press through the ceiling for any hint of what might be going on with Gram. She tried to understand what had happened, why Gram so willingly left with Sister Mary, and if that thing from the rift had actually called Gram *Mom*.

CHAPTER 3

Once Roni made it clear that she would remain in the cellar, Sister Claudia sent Sisters Susan and Rachel upstairs. Sister Claudia then returned to the bookstands to start her inspection. As if she had been slapped by a loved one, the sudden change in the moment hit Roni. She gawked, frozen, her face locked in an incredulous stare. Sister Claudia adjusted an ornate wooden stand before gazing over at Roni.

With her hands on her hips, Sister Claudia said, "Is this your first time ever seeing a rift?"

With a dazed shake of her head, Roni said, "What? No. I've seen them several times. Not like this one, but I've seen them."

"Then stop acting like a child and get over here."

A headache emanated from her tight brow. She rubbed her forehead, trying to lose her frown, as she walked over to the books. In all the excitement, Roni had never taken the time to look at the books or their stands with a close eye. And though she could process the information now — each of them being different, some beautifully carved, some metallic and some utilitarian — her mind swirled like the rift.

"Did you see her?" Roni asked.

Sister Claudia kept her attention on the books. "I've seen that girl many times."

"In the rift? That girl who pushed outward and stared at me?" *And stared at Gram.*

Resetting a book with more force the necessary, Sister Claudia said, "Yes. I have seen that girl in the rift. Why is this so difficult to understand?"

"Who is she?"

"One of the Lord's chosen, of course."

"Excuse me?"

Sister Claudia strolled around the circle with her hands behind her back like a schoolmarm until she reached Roni. "I know the stories you tell each other in the Parallel Society. I've read accounts in our library about you all. But this rift is not another universe. There is no other universe. There is only the one made by the Lord. And this, the passage, this marvelous gift to us, the Sisters of Croghan Abbey, this is a conduit."

"A conduit?"

"For several generations now, the Sisters have stood vigil here, open to the glorious light of our Lord above. Through this conduit he sends his messengers."

Sister Claudia returned to the bookstands and placed a Bible on the second tier beneath the books from the Parallel Society. As if sitting a baby into a highchair, she set the Bible gently down. Her hand pressed against the cover with a soft touch. Then, with great care and kindness, she wrapped a silk ribbon around the book, tying it to the stand.

"You think this rift leads to Heaven?" Roni said.

"When these books are properly aligned, yes. But as you saw, when we fail in our duty, it opens a terrible, vengeful wrath. I don't dare utter the name of that place."

Roni's eyes snatched a glance upward. She needed to speak with Gram and hope her grandmother would be more forthcoming than usual. "That girl. The one that looks like a young version of me —"

"Did she?" Sister Claudia took a moment to observe Roni's face. "Perhaps."

Roni halted as pieces of the conversation snapped together. "If this rift is a way to connect with Heaven, and the girl is one of the Lord's messengers, then you're saying—"

"Ay, she's an angel."

The Sister's eyes sparkled as her words hung in the air. Roni struggled to keep her face from betraying her thoughts. What kind of angel would reach out to Gram and call her *Mom?* The way the Sisters treated this rift, the way Sister Claudia spoke of it, wriggled along Roni's spine. She shook her head. They were zealots.

Gesturing to the books, Sister Claudia said, "Anytime you're ready."

"Sorry." Roni got to work inspecting each one of the Parallel Society books, making sure they did their part to dampen the rift, searching for any errors or signs that a book might fail. When she finished, she would be able to talk with Gram, get some real answers, and get out of this place.

Sister Claudia followed her as she worked around the circle. "You're not much of a Christian are you?"

"Gram raised me in your faith, but it didn't take."

"That's okay. I think you'll feel different when you leave today."

"Doubt it."

"I know. I was like you — not exactly, of course, but I had my doubts." Sister Claudia's voice softened and her hard glares eased. "Even when I became a nun, I had my doubts. In fact, for the first four years, I prayed and prayed until my hands grew calloused from the rosaries and my legs were black and blue from kneeling for so long. I figured if the Lord wanted me to keep following this path, He would see how fervently I prayed and perhaps he would give me some sign or feeling or something to help me find my faith.

"I even reached the point that I was about to leave. I absolutely cannot stand hypocrisy. Makes me want to scream. So, there was no way I would be a hypocrite myself. If I did not have the faith flowing through me to my core, then I had no choice but to find some other calling in life.

"But then Sister Mary came my way.

"She brought me here with a promise — that I would only have to take one look and all my faith would be restored. Of course, she brought me down here. And as you can see, the veil is lifted here. This is the truth floating before you — there is my life before having seen the truth and now my life after.

"It's strange knowing that almost everyone in the world goes through their days with no proof that there really are angels, that there really is a Heaven. They have faith. Many have great depths of faith. But we at the Croghan Abbey — we are the chosen few. We stand before this great conduit to Heaven. We protect it. And we see the Angel. It is the greatest honor I could ever ask for and I would never dream of going back to the way my life had been."

Roni stopped next to a stone bookstand. "Why are you telling me this?"

"Because you should know that you are always welcome back. The Lord forgives, and so do we."

Roni suspected that Sister Claudia's warm openness

would turn brutally cold if she were refuted. Nonetheless, it was tempting. But Roni kept her mouth closed. Especially because much of what the Sister said rang true. Not the religious angle — Roni remained an atheist through and through — but the larger ideas sounded too familiar. The way Sister Claudia split her life into a time before learning the truth and a time after. That reminded Roni too much of her own experience. And like the Sister, Roni could not conceive of returning to a time when she did not know the truth of the Parallel Society.

Am I a zealot? she wondered.

Before she could ask Sister Claudia any further questions, footsteps on the stairs announced the arrival of Sister Susan. She entered carrying a bloody rag that she dabbed at her nose. She bowed slightly and did not move until Sister Claudia spoke.

"Well?" Sister Claudia said.

"Sister Mary is in the dorm. She asked that I inform the young lady that she may see her grandmother now."

Before Sister Susan had finished speaking, Roni bolted for the stairs.

CHAPTER 4

Roni's heart pounded when she reached the top of the stairs — from the exertion and the anticipation of seeing Gram. She banged open the door leading outside and headed for the nun's dorm. Halfway across the grass, she heard Gram's distinctive voice.

"Over here."

Roni glanced at the colonnade between the dorm and the church. Gram rested her elbows on the railing and held a shot glass in her hand. Roni hurried over. "Are you okay?" she asked.

Gram knocked back the last of her drink. "Got a little rattled, that's all. Holding back that rift takes quite a lot out of you — especially at my age."

Roni wanted to barrel into the questions bouncing around her head, but Gram looked too vulnerable, too shaken. Putting out her hand, Roni said, "Come here. Let me help you. We can go for a walk. Clear our heads."

Gram paused to look at her empty glass. She set it on the ground before clasping Roni's hand and gracelessly swinging her leg over the railing. She giggled as she stumbled onto the grass.

"How many shots of you had?" Roni asked.

"Oh, phooey. Enough to relax, that's all. I'm not drunk. I just thought that the sight of me flying over that railing and nearly falling on my rear was funny. And don't you dare start acting judgmental towards me. I'm still your grandmother. Show some respect."

"There's the Gram I know." They headed across the circle, onto the grass, and toward the wide lake. A gravel path followed the perimeter of the lake, and they decided to walk the entire way around. Glancing back at the church, Roni said, "Did that nun try to do anything with you? Say anything to you?"

"What would she try to do?"

"I don't know. You're the one who told me to be careful around them, not to trust them."

Gram rubbed Roni's shoulder. "I've known Sister Mary longer than you've been alive. She has a good heart and strong faith."

"Then why shouldn't I trust her?"

"Because these women can get kind of nutty. They don't believe the rift leads to another universe."

"I heard that story from Sister Claudia. She really thinks they have a special telephone to Heaven. But more than that is going on here. Come on. I know you. You wouldn't have told me not to trust them if it was something as benign as them being religious fruitcakes."

"Even the dumbest of religious beliefs can spawn horrible and dangerous people." Gram paused. She bent down, picked up a stone, and tossed it into the water. As the ripples expanded out, she said, "Out here, life is slow and still and calm. Except for that rift. These women have all been here too long. I've seen them come in, young and eager, full of faith and hope and a desire to do good in the world. But being near that thing changes them. That doesn't mean I can't be kind to an old woman like Sister Mary — I can even be fond of her — but it does mean that we have to be careful around them."

"The rift changes them? How?"

Linking her arm through Roni's, Gram strolled along the path again. "I've never been able to discover exactly what was going on, but I've seen the change and I can sense it. Sully and Elliot have always assumed it was negative effects from the energy pulsing out of that rift. I suppose."

"Well, the books are secure on their stands again and that rift isn't going anywhere. No matter how much wind it blows."

"That wasn't the rift. At least, I've never seen it act so violently. It's frighteningly calm, usually."

"But all that wind and the horrible sounds."

"Those are from the books we put in place. This may sound strange to you, but they are full of negative energy which sort of forces the rift to hold still. The books kind of cower the rift."

"Is that why the nuns think it leads to Heaven? Because the Society books are negative energy, they think the rift must be positive?"

"Oh, I will never claim to comprehend the minds of these nuns."

Roni discarded the further questions filling her mind. "The job is done. That's what matters. We can go back to the car and take the first flight out of here."

Gram gave Roni's arm a squeeze. "I wish it were that simple."

She pulled away and walked to the edge of the lake. With her head bowed toward the water, she clasped her crucifix, closed her eyes, and prayed. Roni waited. She had thought that once they were on the plane, she would be able to pry loose some relevant information about the girl in the rift, but between the praying and the drinking, she saw that this had hit Gram like a quake from within.

Roni came alongside her grandmother. When Gram finished praying, they watched each other through their reflections. The water distorted them.

With a defeated smile, Gram said, "You might as well ask me now."

"If I ask you, will you tell me the truth?"

"I have no choice. Not just because lying is a sin, but because you need to know. You'll be coming out here year after year for the rest of your life. You need to know what you're dealing with."

Roni walked back to where the grassy ground sloped upward. She sat and smoothed a section next to her. When Gram came over and settled in, Roni said, "Okay, then — what's the story about that girl? Why did she call you *Mom*? Did you have another daughter or what?"

Gram raised her hand to silence Roni. "You only had to ask the question one way."

"Sorry. I'm just a bit —"

She splayed out her fingers and stopped Roni again. "I suppose it's merely wishful thinking that you will ever learn patience. Lord knows I prayed to Him enough, and it hasn't happened yet." Gram glanced over her shoulder, back toward the church, and sniffled. "Doesn't look like much from afar. Sometimes, it's hard to believe so much of my life has changed in that building."

Roni stopped herself from pressing further. The woman was building up the courage to speak. Roni sat on her hands and clinched her teeth together. *Patience,* she warned herself.

"First off, you do not have an aunt," Gram said. "Maria was my only daughter as you were her only daughter. The reason that girl in the rift looks so much like you, the reason she called me Mom, is because she is also my daughter, Maria." She pressed her palms against her eyes and shuddered. Seeing Gram push back her tears kept Roni quiet a little longer. Gram went on, "I raised your mother with a full knowledge of the Parallel Society and her eventual role in it. I wanted her to be prepared, to be skilled, so that there would be a smooth transition when I retired. So, when Maria, your mother, turned twelve years old, I decided to bring her with me here — to Croghan Abbey.

"I was very proud. Partly of her — she braved the unknown with such confidence that I always felt the Parallel Society would be in great hands with her. But I also had arrogant pride in myself. Maria's successes spoke to my great parenting — or so I thought.

"It was early-Spring when we came here. I remember that because the grass smelled incredibly alive and it was so vividly green. I understood why so many fairy tales came from this part of the world. It was like walking through a painting still wet and fresh.

"Sister Mary had joined the church only a handful of years earlier, but she and I had become friends quickly. She fawned over Maria, acting as if she were more than a family friend. She was Auntie Mary, and she happily paraded Maria in front of all the other nuns. There was lots of cooing and pinching of cheeks and all sorts of silly behavior. Like I said, I was arrogantly proud. And I think Maria knew it, too. At least, she knew she was getting great heaps of attention, even if she didn't understand the full implications of why.

"Time came to get to work, so I took her by the hand and walked down the spiral staircase and brought her to the rift. I felt so full of myself. I'd impressed the nuns by showing off my daughter, and now, I intended to impress my daughter by showing off the rift. I got to work inspecting the books, and at first, everything proceeded wonderfully.

"But my pride had blinded me. I forgot that Maria did not know everything she needed to know – did not know the rules. She understood the basics of the Parallel Society, but that did not qualify her to do anything more than observe. And I failed to caution her. Out of curiosity and a desire to help, she stepped forward — and this I will never forget — she smiled at me."

With a bitter grin, Gram stroked Roni's face. "There's a specific way a child looks at her parents when she wants to show off how much she can do. It's more than pride, more than a desire for acceptance, more than simple precociousness. It's all of those things but it's also a question — a simple idea — a child wants to show that she can do Good."

Roni gripped the grass under her hands to keep from shaking her head. She understood exactly what was going through her mother's head. Maria did not want to show off or receive praise or even do Good. She wanted to feel useful. "She picked up one of the books, didn't she?"

"She wanted her mother to know that she was learning, that she would soon be ready, that she understood the importance of what the Parallel Society does, but she didn't understand. I mean, she knew that the books were dangerous, Lord knows I drilled that into her all the time, but she had no idea that this rift was so drastically different than those in the caverns under the bookstore. She lifted the book with caution and care. But that wasn't enough.

"These books — they radiate out energy at a specific frequency. It's the negative to the rift's positive. It's how they keep the rift from expanding. But the one Maria picked up had lost its ability to hold together. Spending years pushing against this rift causes the books extreme wear. She held that book in her hands and the spine tore apart."

Gram stared out at the lake as if she could see the events unfold in the air before her. "It struck out so fast. Like a snake sinking its teeth into a victim. No wind. No roars or growls or anything that we've come to expect from another universe. I have no idea how I reacted so quickly myself, but as that thing pulled Maria towards it, I whipped out a chain. I had it wrapped twice around Maria's wrist." Gram dabbed her eyes once more. "Maria cried out. Unbridled screams — the way only a child can scream in terror. She sounded so loud in the quiet of the room. I threw out another chain. Got around her waist that time. And I pulled. I could feel my muscles moving beyond their capacity. I could feel my bones digging into the ground. I screamed so hard my throat ached for three days. I was determined to save that girl — *my* girl. I suppose all mothers go through that when their child is in jeopardy, but this wasn't anything human beings evolved to be able to do. This was me protecting my daughter from being pulled into another universe.

"Seven chains. In the end, it took me seven chains to pull her out. But I did. She cried and cried in my arms, scared and shaking, she even wet herself, and I did not care because she was in my arms, and that was all that mattered."

Roni wriggled her hand free. "If you saved her, then who did we see in the rift?"

"When we got back home, I could tell she was proud of herself. Not only had she gone on her first outing to another country, but she had faced another universe and survived. Except there were little things — things that felt off.

"Pretty soon, these little things, small differences, started adding up. It was one thing for her to suddenly like strawberries when she never liked them before. Or the way she didn't mind using the bathroom on the plane, while in the past, she had been particular about only going to the bathroom at home. I could dismiss these as the natural changes of a girl growing up. But then as the year progressed, her behavior became stranger. She was more aggressive, more disobedient, and very much became the wild child that you knew as your mother."

"Isn't that called *being a teenager?*"

"I thought so, too. For the longest time. But when all the changes were put together, I saw that she was not the same. I still did not know what had really happened. I still thought I'd saved her. But a few years later, during my regular visit to the Abbey to inspect the books, Sister Mary beamed with pride. She confessed to me that the Abbey had finally been vindicated in their faith. The rift let them see into Heaven. They had been visited by an angel."

"Maria."

"The rift had split her. The girl that had returned with me, that grew up and became your mother, that Maria had been formed from the impulsive side of her. The other side of her, the risk averse side, the caring and selfless side, remains trapped in the rift — stuck at the same age and, presumably, in that same moment."

Roni launched forward and rushed down the hill to the edge of the lake. Her fingers made small circles at her temples as blood pounded through her head. Gram heaved a sob from behind, but it sounded miles away.

Roni's thoughts swirled together and spun off in all directions. She tried to hold the concept of her mother split in two, but it kept slipping away. Part of her brain felt as if she had walked out into the lake and submerged under its icy waters. The rest of her raged so fiery-hot that she would boil the lake if she touched it.

Whirling back upon Gram, Roni said, "You've known this my whole life, yet you let me think I'd lost everything. You let me think my mother died in that car accident."

"She did." Gram's brow tightened as did her mouth. "This splitting of Maria happened long before you were even so much as a thought. The Maria I returned home with, the one I raised, the one who liked to drink too much, liked men too much, liked drugs too much — that was your mother. That was the woman who held you in her womb for nine months, and that was the woman who gave birth to you. No other."

"It never ends with you. One secret leads to another and another."

"Oh, grow up. Everybody has secrets."

"Not about the nature of the entire universe. And not about their granddaughter's mother being splintered off into two beings." Roni inhaled a long, sharp breath and tried to calm down. Her mind threatened to attack Gram again — this time striking at the religious angle. But that would only provoke the woman and would close any opportunity to get more information.

Gram shuffled down the hill. "I truly am sorry. This has been a stain upon my entire life. I've prayed endlessly about this. Perhaps I should have told you. I don't know what good it would've done, but perhaps I should have. I just ... I'm ashamed."

Roni glanced away. She wanted to punch things. She wanted to rage. But seeing the distraught, broken look in Gram's eyes mollified the urge. Her fingers opened and her mind eased.

"You didn't know," she said. "Not until you saw Mom's behavior back home, and by that point, it was too late."

"I should've tried to save her when I came back here that next year. When Sister Mary started talking about angels, I knew it was my Maria in there. I wouldn't actually see here for a few more years, but I knew. I just didn't want to believe it."

Roni reached over and stroked Gram's cheek with the back of her hand. "We're here now, and we just saw her. It's not too late. We should go save her."

Gram's face turned to stone. "That's the worst possible idea." She pulled away as if stepping back from a horrid monster. "You must promise me to never do that. Do you not recall what happened only a few years ago? The thing that brought you into all of this? When your boyfriend went into one of my books and came out a different being altogether."

"He was not my boyfriend."

"We have no idea what the universe inside that rift is like. But we do know it's kept that version of Maria frozen in time. She's not aged in all the years I've come here. Lord knows what that experience would do to her brain, her psyche. You understand? Bringing her back now might destroy all that she has left. It would also unleash an unknown creature into our world. She is no longer from this universe. To bring her here would be like bringing anything from another universe here — she would be a living relic, and those are not allowed. Too unpredictable. The foreign germs alone could be devastating to our world."

"You think your daughter is a relic?"

Gram's mouth became a small dot. "That Maria is no longer my daughter. And she most certainly is not your mother."

"I only meant —"

With a wave of her hand, Gram thumped off toward the

church. "I need to report in to Sully."

Roni watched as Gram walked away. Clenching her fists, Roni kicked the gravel path. She grabbed handfuls of rocks and tossed them into the lake. She threw her arms in the air and let out an exasperated cry.

How could Gram be so blind? Roni understood how horrible an experience the whole thing must have been — her only daughter, split in two, partly lost in another universe, with no way to return. Gut wrenching. But like so much that came out of Gram's mouth, that wasn't the entire truth.

Because Gram ignored the possibility of saving her daughter. She wrote off the split and focused on the living daughter she still had. But that did not change the truth — the Maria in the rift was still Gram's daughter, and in a sense, still Roni's mother. Partly, anyway. Gram's woes concerning the unpredictability of the rift did not negate the need to, at the least, attempt a rescue. Further proof that Gram no longer had the capacity to lead the group.

Perhaps Sully had assigned Roni this job because of Maria. If Sully knew about the situation — and Roni thought all three in the Old Gang knew everything about each other — then it could not have been an accident that he sent her alongside Gram. He wanted her to learn about Maria.

And that means part of my job must be to save her.

Roni stopped mid-step. She turned back and looked at the church spire peeking over the hilltops. Sister Claudia had mentioned a library. If this group of nuns behaved anything like the Parallel Society, then they would have accounts left behind by previous nuns. Somebody had to have written down something of value regarding Maria. After all, the appearance of this rift and then years later their so-called Angel had to have been the most monumental event in the Abbey.

With a more determined step, Roni headed back toward the church. She had to find Sister Claudia and gain access to that library. She had to save Maria.

CHAPTER 5

Roni found Sister Claudia tending to the flower beds that lined the circle drive. After everything that had happened, Roni found it peculiar that Sister Claudia would perform such a mundane task. Then again, Roni spent most of her days working in a bookstore that had the caverns leading to other universes beneath it. She supposed living with the rift bore many of the same results — the nuns had become comfortable with their situation and learned to continue living despite the miracle beneath their church.

Roni asked about the library, and Sister Claudia wasted no time leaving behind her backbreaking work. She led the way to the colonnade and building on the opposite side of where Roni had found Gram only a short while earlier. The building appeared to have been built in the 1960s — utilitarian, mostly red brick with narrow windows, and a flat roof. In style, it reminded Roni of a public high school. Inside the library, however, she discovered a far more ancient atmosphere.

Dim lighting and old wood shrouded the aisles of books with a sense of mystery and importance. Off to her right, Roni noted long wide shelves that carried scrolls covered in dust. Rolling ladders provided access to the numerous volumes on the top shelving — must have been about twenty-feet high. In the middle of this ode to lost and forgotten thoughts, a young nun sat in the center of a donut table.

"This is Sister Ashley," Sister Claudia said. "And this is Roni. She is one of our guests from the Parallel Society."

Sister Ashley bowed her head. She had a pert nose and smooth skin, and Roni wondered if such features caused jealousy amongst the nuns. Perhaps being cloistered in a nun's habit and coif actually dispensed with all that physical nonsense. Perhaps out here, these women could simply treat each other based on their intelligence, their faith, and their abilities.

"It's a pleasure to meet you," Sister Ashley said in a soft voice. "Is there something I can help you with?"

Roni asked for any writings the nuns had made about the rift. In particular, she wanted information on the angel. As Sister Ashley got to work, Sister Claudia gestured to two tables in the back where they could sit down to do their research.

"You want to help me?" Roni asked.

"It's far more enjoyable than weeding. Besides, Sister Mary told me to give you aid in any way you needed. So, here I am."

Shortly after, Sister Ashley deposited three books and one scroll on the work tables in the back. Roni had been hoping for more, but she guessed that regardless of faith, belief in conduits to Heaven or angels manifesting in physical form were still dangerous things to write down. The kinds of things that might make the Vatican no longer recognize an entire Abbey.

She grabbed one of the thick books — its dusty leather cover caused her a short coughing fit — and opened to the table of contents. The pages were thin enough to see shadows through and the print so small and tight that she considered asking Sister Ashley for a magnifying glass.

Sister Claudia chuckled. "Not what you were expecting?"

"I hadn't given it any thought. I just want to do the research."

"Of course. Discovering the truth is always a noble endeavor. I assume that's what you're after."

Roni hesitated to answer. She thought of Gram's warning and of the devotion Sister Claudia had displayed toward the Abbey. She might not have taken it kindly that Roni wanted to grab hold of their angel and remove it from the rift. Worse, Roni wanted to take this angel home with her.

"Something a bother?" Sister Claudia asked.

With a shake of her head, Roni started going through the book.

Sister Claudia tipped back her chair and with a nonchalant motion, swiped one of the other books. She leafed through it in a casual way as if passing over the endless advertisements in a fashion magazine. "I know you think we're all a little nutters here. Oh look, how quaint. The young, foolish nuns in the backwoods of Ireland are talking with the angels. But I think that's not anymore crazy then what you're believing."

Roni paused. "The rift is a hole between universes — that's not a belief, that's a fact. And I've been through one of them. I can guarantee you, it was no Heaven."

"Just because your travels took you to a horrible place, does not mean our conduit does not lead to Heaven."

"You only believe that because you saw a face in there, and you think it's an angel."

"And your grandmother thinks it's her daughter. She has

no proof. If anything, she has the opposite — her daughter lived, went home with her, grew to be an adult and have a child of her own. I think your grandmother can't get her heart over the loss of her innocent daughter, the way her daughter succumbed to sin, and has projected this idea of a perfect daughter she once thought she had onto our angel. Perhaps the Lord has given the angel a similar face to ease your grandmother's sorrowed heart. After all, despite your mother's sinful behavior, despite your own rejection of the Church, your grandmother is still a devout believer. The Lord loves her."

Roni gripped the edge of the table. "I think it would be best if you left me alone for a while. I can do this research on my own."

Sister Claudia stood with a shrug. "If that's what you are thinking's best."

As she walked away, Roni rose to her feet. "Sister Claudia, you've accidentally taken one of my books with you."

Sister Claudia glanced down as if only discovering the book in her hands. "This? I looked through it already. It will not help you."

"Still, if you don't mind."

Though Sister Claudia's mouth lifted in a smile, pure venom dripped from her gaze. "Unfortunately, Sister Ashley made a mistake when she brought this book out. Not all of our texts are available for you to touch." She shot a narrow glare at Sister Ashley.

"I'm sorry, ma'am," Sister Ashley said with a motion somewhere between a bow and a curtsy.

Roni tapped the desk. "I certainly understand how precious some rare books can be. I also understand that because I'm not part of your faith, you don't want me looking through certain texts. But Sister Ashley is also a nun here. Perhaps she can help."

"I doubt that our young librarian knows —"

"Or maybe we can call upon Sister Mary for advice in this matter. I'm sure she's hanging out with Gram right now."

Sister Claudia bristled. "Sister Mary doesn't need to be bothered with this kind of nonsense. She trusts me to be in charge, and so you'll have to take my word for this decision. You don't need this book."

She started to walk off again, but Roni said, "It sucks, doesn't it? Sister Mary tells you that you're going to be head of this place one day, but she doesn't really give you the trust you deserve."

"Do not try to equate your petty little problems with those that I face," Sister Claudia said, stopping but not turning back.

"They might be petty, but if you don't allow me to look at that book, I'll have no choice. I've got a job to do. So, if I must, I'll go to Sister Mary myself. Now, maybe you're right. Maybe she'll agree that you made the correct decision, and she'll throw me out of here. Perhaps her decades-long relationship with my grandmother means nothing to her. Then again, and I'm only posing the possibilities, but perhaps she'll tell you that you're wrong. That Gram and I are here to ensure this rift doesn't destroy everything. From that standpoint, it's important that we have all the information available."

Huffing, Sister Claudia slammed the book on Sister Ashley's desk. Pointing a strong finger at Sister Ashley, she said, "Don't think I don't know what you're up to. It was no mistake that this book was in her pile. If any harm comes of this, I will hold you responsible."

Before Sister Ashley could mumble her apologies, Sister Claudia stomped out of the library. Roni stepped forward to glimpse at the book cover — an ornate illustration of two priests putting a body to rest. The cover's border had an intricate design of thorns and stems ending in roses. The title of the book — *The Abbey Tombs*.

"I'm sorry if I caused you any trouble," Roni said, trying to look closer.

Sister Ashley picked up the book and returned to the worktable. "Not at all." She peeked toward the exit, apparently looking for Sister Claudia. With no sign of the woman returning, Sister Ashley said, "In fact, Sister Claudia is right. I did put this book on your pile on purpose. I've always had an interest in the angel and the conduit, but more than that, what really fascinates me are the Abbey tombs. And I'm certain that there are answers to your questions down there."

A jolt of excitement electrified Roni's fingers. "The tombs? What exactly —"

"Let me show you." Sister Ashley opened the book and rifled through the pages with none of the care a librarian should have for such a delicate artifact. When she reached the desired page, she slapped her hand to the top of it and said, "There. Look at that."

Roni leaned over the volume — the rich aroma of old, molding paper rose around her. The text was difficult to read — the handwritten script showed little care for legibility. Plus, Roni figured it was written in Gaelic or Celtic or some other variant, none of which she knew. But there was no mistaking the illustration — a single figure, a nun, flat on her back like an Egyptian Pharaoh, with an oversized book clutched in her arms.

"What's it say?" Roni asked, the catch in her throat unmistakable.

Whispering, Sister Ashley said, "This was Sister Agnes. And the book she was buried with is called *History of Secrets*.

She couldn't have been more on the nose with that." Sister Ashley's face broadened like a hungry wolf. "I've always wanted to see it, but we aren't allowed in the tombs. Sister Mary goes down there once or twice a year, but otherwise, I've never seen a single nun go there."

Roni nodded. She understood the game they were about to play. "So, if I understand this, the rule is that you are not to go down there?"

"That's correct."

"But Sister Claudia told you to help me."

"That is also correct."

"Sister Claudia is working under orders from Sister Mary — the nun who runs this place."

"Ay."

"And in order for you to help me, I need to see that book — *History of Secrets*."

Sister Ashley tapped her chin in a studious manner. "Why then, I suppose the only way to do that would be to take you down there."

"It seems like the only logical action you have available. I hate to ask you to break a rule, but you have a choice to make — you can break the one rule about the tombs, or you can break Sister Claudia's rule about helping me which also breaks Sister Mary's rule."

Sister Ashley nodded so fast and with such a wide smile, Roni wondered if her teeth might crash together. "It seems I'd best break one rule rather than two."

"If you think that's best. Then, please, lead the way. We would be better off taking care of this as fast as possible."

"Oh, indeed. If Sister Claudia were to return, then she would not let us go down there."

"Which means she would be breaking Sister Mary's order to help me and the Parallel Society. We don't want to put her in that position."

"Not at all."

Sister Ashley gathered the books together and set them on her desk. Neither woman said another word. Roni followed Sister Ashley's lead and they headed for the tombs.

CHAPTER 6

The Abbey tombs were comprised of several twisting passageways built underneath the library. Narrow and rough, they reminded Roni of certain sections of the caverns under the bookstore — the ones that had been carved out by hand. Like all of Ireland, the air felt damp and cold.

As Sister Ashley led the way by flashlight, Roni noticed long alcoves dug into the walls. Each one contained a gray, dusty skeleton draped in habit, wimple, tunic, and in some cases, armor.

"Are these all nuns?" she asked.

"Hush."

"But if they're nuns, shouldn't we be checking —"

Sister Ashley spun around, blinding Roni with the flashlight. "You best be quiet or you're going to get us caught." Her eyes darted toward one of the bodies. "Besides, it's wrong to be talking like this amongst the dead." Without another word, she resumed leading the way.

Roni considered pressing the issue, but in the end, she had to trust that Sister Ashley knew where to go. Thankfully, the majority of the bodies were difficult to discern in the dark shadows. Though the occasional skull smiling at her was more than enough to chill her bones. Worse, the air smelled stale and left Roni's mouth with a dry coating — she didn't want to think about that too much.

They came upon a heavy door with an iron ring for the handle. From beneath her habit, Sister Ashley produced a key that looked as old as the church itself. It took her five tries to get the door unlocked — the results of frayed nerves and an ancient lock.

She had to put her shoulder into the door hard in order to force it open. It obliged with a long and horrible whine as if it wanted to send waves of eerie sound across the dead. Roni glanced back into the dark and dusty shadows. If she heard a deep moan or even the squeak of a rat, she thought she would be justified in letting out a sharp scream.

"Come on," Sister Ashley whispered. "We're not down here for a show. Let's get this done."

Roni nodded and followed the nun through the door. They entered a narrow, low-ceilinged room — a private study. A plain, wooden desk and an equally plain, wooden chair had been pressed up against one wall. Next to these, a wood-frame bed with three thick blankets upon a rope lattice served as a place to sleep. On the wall opposite, two columns of shelves contained bodies on the left side and books on the right. A narrow, blackened fireplace comprised the back corner. Dark stains on the ceiling suggested a lack of adequate ventilation.

Sister Ashley centered her flashlight on the bed. "Sister Agnes lived here. The legend is that after she experienced the conduit for the first time — for the only time — she sequestered herself down here to write all her musings on what she had seen. Back then, nobody dared to say the truth — that she had glimpsed Heaven."

"Back when? How long ago did all this happen?"

"Seventeenth century, I think." She turned her flashlight toward the shelves of books and scrolls. "These are my favorite. They detail all kinds of things about life back then. It sounds wonderfully peaceful. I wouldn't mind living without electricity, but not having modern plumbing is something hard to idealize. But I can imagine life without all the noise of today. Sister Agnes did more than write about the world she lived in, though. More than just her experience with the conduit, too. She took the time to talk about her own spirituality. Very inspiring."

Roni cocked her head to the side. "I thought you hadn't been down here before."

"I said that I wasn't allowed to come down here. Not that I've never been here."

It sounded reasonable, but Roni did not recall the conversation going that way originally.

Woooooo. A horrible sound, like poorly played bagpipes, echoed around them. *Wooooo.* Roni's skin prickled.

Sister Ashley pointed to a row of evenly-spaced holes in the ceiling, each one circled by black residue that then trailed back to the fireplace. "Ventilation. Sister Agnes would have died long before she did without a trickle of fresh air coming her way. You should hear this place when a good rainstorm blows through. You can hear that sound all throughout the tombs."

Roni's gaze drifted across the bare room. She thought about Sister Agnes being down here amongst the dead and how bizarre the others must have thought her. That led to thoughts about the nuns, the Church, and —

"What is it you're thinking?" Sister Ashley asked.

With an embarrassed turn of her head, Roni said, "I'm not sure how to ask this politely."

"Then I'd recommend being honest."

"In that case, how did you end up here?"

Sister Ashley laughed. "You mean how did a nice nun like me end up in a place like this?"

Chuckling, Roni nodded.

"I imagine my story is much like all the other nuns here — at least, those that came after Sister Mary. Like most, I came to it because I had a moment — a calling. I grew up on a farm in County Kilkenny. I was not a wild one, always acted a proper child, but I wasn't particularly religious and I didn't listen to my parents well when I was involved in something. Mostly, I loved the books, and when I got to reading, I never heard a single thing my parents would say."

Sister Ashley's brightness faltered. "My father — he was a stricter sort. Spare the rod and all that. The way he went at me, my sister, and my brothers, well, I suppose I could have understood it if we were fussy or causing troubles. But we were good kids. And we were smart. Smart enough not stick around and get beaten for nothing. So, we left. Well, I did, anyway.

"I ended up on the streets of Galway which is not a place you want to end up. I saw so many other kids succumb to drugs and prostitution, and I was determined that would not happen to me. I tried getting jobs, I tried begging, I tried anything — but I always ended up sleeping in an alley.

"One day I was standing by the water watching the tide, and there were other people walking around during the day. There was a man — odd-looking fellow with a crooked nose and a long face. He caught my eye and I watched him walking along. He carried this packet of papers, and I assumed he was handing out adverts for some pub or something, but he didn't hand them out to anybody. He watched everyone and just walked right by.

"Until he came to me.

"He stopped and stared at me, and I got the strange feeling inside like he could see through all the walls I had built up from living on the streets. He handed me the paper and walked away. It was a call to church. The whole thing felt so strange that I decided to go. I walked in there and I listen to that service, and it changed me. If you've never had a calling, you can't possibly know what it feels like. And if you've had one, then I don't need to explain. It hit me then. I would give my life to the Lord. And I did."

"If you felt that strongly," Roni said, "why did you stay here when this abbey was rejected by the Church?"

"Why would I stay with a church that rejects a pathway to Heaven itself? That's like rejecting the Lord. Why would any of us do that? The real question you should be asking is why didn't more of our brethren join us here? That's what I want." Gesturing to the corpse of Sister Agnes, Sister Ashley said, "She understood. She saw that conduit and sequestered herself here and devoted her life here to the Lord. That's what I want to do. That's what all of us nuns want to do. We are here to serve the Lord. We are chosen, and I would give up everything to remain here. No Vatican, no Pope, no father or mother or friend could beat me or sway me because after all — what was my calling if not to serve the Lord? And He has provided us with this conduit to His Heaven."

Roni had never seen such firm conviction blaze in the eyes of a person. It was both impressive and unnerving. "Let's find the book we're here for — *History of Secrets*. Do you know where Sister Agnes is buried? Is she one of these?"

"Wouldn't make much sense to bring you down here if I didn't know where to go." She walked over to the foot of the bed and indicated that Roni should help her move the furniture. It was heavier than Roni had expected, but they managed to pull the bed out about two feet. They had revealed an alcove dug into the wall, and in the alcove, the remains of Sister Agnes waited.

With giddy excitement, Sister Ashley lowered to her knees and reached in. She pulled out a large book — it required both hands to hold and covered her like a shield from chin to waist. "See? The book as promised."

As Sister Ashley set *History of Secrets* on the desk, Roni approached like a hiker discovering a venomous snake in her path. The nun sneezed and waved a hand to disperse the dust climbing up from the book. But to Roni's eyes, the dust came from the desk, not the book. In fact, she thought the book appeared rather clean.

Unlike the books upstairs in the Abbey library, this book had a black cover with a red diamond in the middle. No title, no author, no writing of any kind. No illustrations, either. Just the red diamond.

Roni's throat tightened. She had seen books like this before. The caverns beneath the bookstore back home were filled with them. "Have you ever opened this book?"

Sister Ashley's face reddened. "Oh, no. I'll admit that I've pulled it out from time to time. I've set it on the floor and looked at it, but I promise you that I have never opened it."

"Why not? If you were so eager to read the books down here, then why not open this one?"

"I want to say that I didn't open it out of respect for Sister Agnes. That's true, to some extent. But the real truth is that whenever I go to open it, I feel something — a force from the book, perhaps from within myself. I assume it is the Lord telling me to obey my vows, to stop. So, I stop."

"Until the urge to come down here strikes you again."

"Indeed." She stroked the cover three times before raising her hopeful eyes toward Roni. "But you are here now. From what I understand, you have no faith, so there should be no problem with you opening the book. The Lord won't speak to you."

"Being an atheist doesn't mean I have no faith in anything at all."

"You have no moral code."

"You know, the atheists' moral track record is far better than your own. You may not want to keep casting stones." Roni heard Gram's stern tones creeping into her own voice. She stepped back and took a cleansing breath. "Maybe I should take the book with me and look at it in private. That way your moral quandary won't be a problem."

Sister Ashley stepped in front of the book. "You cannot do that. The book belongs to Sister Agnes. It must remain here."

"No problem. I'll stay down here and read it. Why don't you go upstairs and return to your library duties — I'll come up when I'm done."

As if in answer, the Vienna Boys Choir broke into a beautiful rendition of *Silent Night*. Sister Ashley dug into her robes and fished out a small phone. She tapped at the screen for a moment and the music stopped.

"My alarm," she said. "The dinner bell is tolling. We have to go."

"I don't need dinner. I'll stay and read the book."

"We cannot be absent. And you can't stay here alone. I promise I will bring you back down. I want you to open the book. But not right now." She looked at the phone in her hand. "And please, not a word about this. I only have it because I can't hear the bells from down here. You understand?"

"Oh, I understand perfectly. It's that strong moral code at work."

Sister Ashley's pleading face darkened. With sharp

movements, she set the book back on the bones of Sister Agnes. In an icy tone that sharpened her button nose, she said, "Being down here can be unnerving for some. I'll assume that has led you to speak without thinking. We will go to dinner now. Don't worry — I stand by my word. After all, honesty is part of my moral code. Tomorrow morning, you and your Gram will come by here again before heading out. I will take you down then."

Sister Ashley gestured toward the door and waited until Roni headed out. As they walked through the twisting paths, Roni attempted to memorize each turn. She listened for sound cues and even tried to leave small marks in the old dust. Anything that would help her when she returned.

Because she would return.

After dinner, she would come down by herself and find that room. No way was she going to open the book in front of Sister Ashley — not when she felt certain the book belonged in the caverns of the Parallel Society, not when she knew it led to another universe.

CHAPTER 7

Once they reached the surface, Sister Ashley rushed off to the dorms to prepare for dinner. Roni headed straight for the rental car, going over every step of the path she would have to repeat in order to get to the book. She popped the trunk and went about preparing her "tomb bag."

The trunk did not have much for her to choose from — neither she nor Gram had expected to be in this situation. She could use her phone has a flashlight, provided the battery lasted long enough, but she did not have any good shoes for the job — only a serviceable pair of sneakers. She did have her journal and a pen to record all the important details. That was good enough. She figured the tomb bag would be mostly empty going in, and probably full on her return.

The idea of stealing the book did not sit easily in her stomach, but clearly the nuns had taken the book when they should not have. It belonged to the Parallel Society, and while the Society had let the Abbey use those books necessary to contain the rift, the rest were meant to be returned to the caverns.

"Oh, there you are," Gram said, shuffling out of the

front of the church.

Roni hastened to meet Gram at the stairs. She purposely left the trunk open — less suspicious than if she slammed it shut with a guilty look on her face.

Nonetheless, Gram asked, "What are you doing out here?"

"Looking for a warmer shirt." The lie came effortlessly.

"Don't bother getting it yet. I spoke with Sully. He's asked that we stay for the night to make sure the rift is secure. After what happened to Sisters Susan and Rachel, we don't want to leave with just a cursory inspection. So, you might as well pull everything out. The nuns will provide us each with a room in the dorms."

"Is that normal? To stay overnight?"

Trying to remain neutral but unable to hide true feelings from her tone, Gram said, "I've done this job many times. Either the rift is contained or it's not. There is no middle ground. I told Sully he was being overcautious, that we've taken care of the situation, but he is the leader now. We do what he wants."

"I–I'm sorry." Roni had no idea why the words left her mouth. Perhaps a little guilt nestled under her skin because of her plans for that evening.

"You've got nothing to be sorry about. It's Sully. He's too much of a novice to know the right procedure here, yet too old and set in his ways to simply ask me how I would have done it. Or perhaps he's trying to stamp his own way of doing things on this now. Who knows? Just please get our things and deliver them to the rooms."

"I only meant that —"

But Gram was already walking away. Over her shoulder, the old woman said, "Oh, by the way, Sully and Elliot are already in London. They're on their way over here."

Roni did not say another word. She knew her Gram too

well — Sully and Elliot flying out to London before anything had necessitated their trip would be interpreted as a great insult. But Roni knew Sully well, too. The more she thought about it, the more she felt certain that he had assigned her to this trip not only to learn of the rift and what would be required in the future, but also because he knew the serious nature of Gram's daughter being trapped in the rift. He knew that this particular trip — especially having Roni along — would be hard on Gram. After all, every year Gram traveled here and visited Maria had to be thought of as potentially the last year she would ever see her daughter. As Gram was fond of reminding everyone — she wasn't getting any younger.

Still, Sully and Elliot should not have flown out as further back up. It only irritated Gram more, and Roni had no desire to spend more time with an irritated Gram. Certainly not for the rest of the trip.

On the positive side, Roni had all night ahead of her to get to that book. Grabbing the luggage and the tomb bag, she closed the trunk and headed to the dorms.

Trudging toward the one-story building, Roni kept catching movement out of her peripheral vision. She stopped and stared at the church, the dorm, even turned to face the lake. She saw no one. The wind rustled through the trees, the water rippled on the lake, but she saw no one. Still, she could not shake the sense that somebody watched her.

Sister Claudia most likely — glowering from some distant hiding place, ready to assert her superiority whenever she had the advantage. *Good luck with that,* Roni thought. Sister Claudia would soon find out that Roni did not cower easily.

Inside the dorm, her footsteps made dull thuds on the wooden floor. The place reminded her of a sleepaway camp cabin — only with a heavily religious theme. The main room held eight beds, each sticking straight out from the longer walls. Above each bed's headboard, a crucifix had been affixed and, beneath that, a wooden plaque with the Sister's name. Next to each bed was a low dresser. Bathrooms were off the main entrance, and at the far end, on either side, were two narrow rooms for Gram and Roni. Not much bigger than jail cells.

As she clumped down the middle of the dorm, Roni noticed that every dresser top remained bare and clean. No books, no knickknacks, nothing to distinguish one person from the other. Not even dust. In fact, only the name plaques provided any sense of individuality. She wondered if she had used the wrong word when thinking about them earlier. Instead of *zealot*, perhaps she should have used *cult*.

After resting Gram's bag on the edge of one bed, Roni went to her own jail cell and dropped her main bag on the floor. She did not want to leave her tomb bag in the open, but there was little in the way of hiding places. She glanced up, hoping to find a drop ceiling that she could stash her belongings in. Unfortunately, she saw only simple, open rafters. Really, the only viable places were under the bed or in the low dresser — and neither of those seemed particularly safe.

After a moment, she decided to roll up the small bag and stick it at the bottom of her main bag. While these nuns had clearly broken away from the Church — at least, according to Gram — it seemed a good bet that they would not go rooting through her personal things — at least, if those things were not left in the open.

"It's not much," Sister Ashley said, giving Roni a fright, "but it serves its purpose for a single night."

Roni stared at Sister Ashley, watching as the nun's eyes roved around the room. Nothing would be safe in here.

"Did you want something?"

"I came to fetch you for dinner. Sister Mary, your Gram, and the rest of the nuns have already sat down to eat."

Until dinner had been mentioned this time, Roni had not taken note of the rich aroma rising through the floorboards — meaty and filling. Her stomach grumbled. She stepped toward the door. "Okay, let's go."

But Sister Ashley did not move. She glanced down — perhaps at Roni's bag — and pulled her lips in tight.

Roni motioned toward the door. "I'm ready."

"One thing first. Please, I do not wish to burden you with my troubles, but I hope you'll understand the seriousness of where we went today. I mean, Sister Mary has made the rules quite clear. Sister Claudia, too. And if you should happen to let slip —"

"I won't say anything. As far as I'm concerned, we never went down to the tomb at all. I don't even know that a tomb exists. Okay?"

Sister Ashley's tensions deflated. "Thank you. Bless you."

"You can thank me by taking me to dinner. I'm hungrier than I realized."

With a giggle, Sister Ashley backed out of the narrow room and into the main part of the dorm. As Roni closed the door, she wanted to slide a hair in the jamb or some other simple trick to ensure that the door was not opened during her absence, but she did not have the time to do it. Not with Sister Ashley standing right there.

Together they walked to the main entranceway. Sister Ashley opened a door across from the bathrooms that Roni had missed her first time through. The door led to a narrow staircase that led to a dining area underneath the dorms.

All the nuns and Gram lifted their heads when Roni and Sister Ashley entered. Sister Mary sat at the head of the long table. Sister Claudia sat at her right and Gram at her left. Sisters Susan and Rachel took the next two spots leaving the rest of the table for Sister Ashley and Roni. With choreographed care, Sister Susan stood the moment Roni sat. She hastened to a corner of the room and ladled out a bowl of stew and potatoes from a heavy, deep pot. After placing the bowl before Roni and repeating the dance for Sister Ashley, she returned to her seat.

"Let us pray," Sister Mary said.

The nuns bowed their heads and Gram did as well. Roni lowered her chin a little, but spent most of the next quiet minute watching the rigorous concentration of the nuns. They bobbed their heads as they mouthed their words, the soft swishing of their wimples like a breeze through a field of grass.

Gram's praying lacked all of that vigor and made up for it with serene contemplation. Growing up, Roni had been taught that the prayer before a meal should be used to appreciate the gifts the Lord had provided — particularly, the gift of having a hot meal on the table to eat. She wondered which form of prayer worked best.

"Amen," Sister Mary said, and the nuns responded in kind. Gram crossed herself and kissed her crucifix pendant before lifting her head.

Smartass thoughts aside, Roni found this display to feel like everything else in the Abbey — strict and slightly off. On the surface, several nuns gave thanks for their meal. Nothing particularly odd about that. But it did not sit right. Not only because of the fervent manner in which they prayed, which Roni could dismiss as simply being a different way of doing things, but because of they way it felt like a performance.

Perhaps the rift had warped the nun's minds in ways that Gram and Roni could not fathom. Perhaps always knowing that rift existed nearby felt too much like being watched continuously. Especially considering that the nuns thought of Maria as an angel. Even now, as Roni ate the surprisingly tasty meal, she could feel judgmental eyes upon her — though the nuns never looked her way. She imagined feeling those kinds of looks all the time might drive some of the strange behaviors she had witnessed.

Five minutes into the meal, Roni accepted the idea that the entire dinner would be taken in silence. But in the next moment, Sister Claudia disabused her of that idea.

"So, Roni, were you able to find everything you needed in the library?" she asked with a nasty grin.

Gram perked up. "What were you looking for?"

Startled, Roni coughed on her stew, allowing Sister Claudia to continue. "Oh, your granddaughter has taken a great interest in our angel."

This got Sister Rachel's attention. Like an eager teenager, though one with head wounds wrapped from earlier failures, she looked over at Roni. "Do you think she's real? I was too startled by what happened to see her clearly. I never have."

"Don't bombard our guest," Sister Claudia said — harsh enough that Sister Rachel instantly grew silent and lowered her head.

"Now, now," Sister Mary said. "We must always encourage inquisitive minds. Sister Rachel is excited and that's a good thing."

Gazing down at her meal, Sister Claudia said, "I only wanted to look out for our guest's comfort. I'm sorry."

"Nothing to be sorry for. We all get overeager sometimes. Sister Ashley, what books did you recommend to our guest?"

Sister Ashley squirmed in her seat. Roni could not tell whether her discomfort came from being addressed by the head nun or if she feared she might get in trouble if she said too much of the truth. Probably both.

"Sister Ashley, you've been asked a question," Sister Claudia said, clearly trying to reestablish her position.

Dabbing at her mouth with a napkin, Sister Ashley said, "Well, I chose two books and one scroll. *The Abbey Historical (1800-1900), The Abbey Historical (1900-2000),* and of course, the scroll of Sister Margaret's views on the subject."

Sister Mary appeared pleased. "I've always liked Sister Margaret's views on practically anything. I must say, I'm a bit surprised they're still sitting around as scrolls. Why have we not bound them together into a book?"

"I intend to do so. And now that I know she's a favorite of yours, I'll make it a priority."

"That's a kind thought."

"It would've been done sooner, but there's only one of me in the library."

Sister Mary gazed at the empty spots making up the second half of the table. "It is much more difficult these days to entice women into making their vows. A vow is for life. Quite a commitment." She winked at Gram. "You wouldn't happen to know any women who could use a good education and don't mind devoting their lives to the Lord, do you?"

Gram chuckled. "If I ever come across one, I'll most certainly send her your way."

As the two elder women beamed at each other, Roni wondered if Sister Mary's eyes threw the same daggers that Gram's could throw. With a snap, Sister Mary wagged her finger by her head. Roni could not tell if this was from the woman's genuine excitement over an idea or if she put on a show, but the presentation pulled everyone's attention.

"While Sister Margaret's work is wonderful," Sister Mary

said, "did you consider offering anything from Sister Petra?" As a loud aside to Gram — loud enough for all to hear — Sister Mary went on, "She was a nun visiting from Brazil. Lovely woman. A bit too inquisitive about matters that had long ago been settled, but she did take an interest in our unique situation. Of course, what nun wouldn't? This was before our trouble with the Vatican. But when given the choice between following the Lord or the Church, well, that choice is easy. It's a shame they behave as they do. We have so much to offer the nuns and priests. Think of all the wonder that could fill them if they had a chance to see a real angel. Still, it's difficult for some to understand and accept. Sister Petra, for one, never did quite fit with us."

Sister Ashley said, "I'll be sure to find her book and give it to Roni."

Returning to her food, Sister Mary said, "It doesn't really matter. Just a thought. Besides, it's obvious that Roni hopes to find some secret information about our angel. Perhaps, like her grandmother, she thinks the angel is some part of their late Maria. Isn't that right, Lillian? You think the angel is actually your daughter."

Gram stiffened even as she forced a grin. "Part of my daughter. Yes."

Setting her spoon down, Sister Mary addressed the rest of the table. "I've tried. Over all the years we've known each other, I've tried hard to convince Lillian that our conduit to Heaven is not a private grave for her mourning. But the mind thinks what it wants to. Regardless, we know that the faces inside the conduit are messengers from the Lord — angels. Frankly, I have not seen one in years. They don't come as often. Perhaps the result of something the Parallel Society has done in trying to control matters. Of course, there is no real need to control it. We should let the

Lord's glory spread over all of the world."

Gram cleared her throat. "Need I remind you —"

"Yes, yes. I was merely stating my opinion. I am fully aware of the deal made with the Irish government." She paused, her eyes meeting with the intense focus from many of the nuns. "I suppose you all deserve to hear this. Sister Claudia already knows, but seeing how few of us there are currently, I suppose the rest of you need to understand — we allow the imposition of the Parallel Society, giving them access to the conduit, letting them contain it and such, because in return we gain our privacy out here. Governments can be very difficult — especially when you are forging an honest path that might differ from the more traditional paths. Gaining this privacy is gaining our freedom. Without it, the Church would come in here and destroy everything we protect. They would not do it out of malice but ignorance."

Sister Claudia said, "We gain more than that. We've become the most important Abbey in the world. We're the only ones that can talk directly to Heaven."

"True, true. But we don't want to get big headed about it. We have to watch our pride."

"Of course."

Gram pushed her chair out. "I'm afraid I'm no longer feeling well. I'll see you all in the morning."

As she made a rapid exit, Roni jumped to her feet. Gram waved her back, and in the next instant, she was gone. Roni returned to the table with the nuns. She had to remain. If not for decorum's sake — something she cared little about — then for the benefit of the Parallel Society. If the nuns made any decisions or shared any thoughts with each other, somebody from the Society needed to hear it. Not that she expected anything important to happen, but if it did and she missed it while Gram was out — she would never hear the end of it.

Sister Claudia snapped her fingers and Sister Rachel went about clearing Gram's dishes. "I'm sorry if we upset your grandmother."

"She's a tough woman," Roni said. "I doubt anything you said could bother her."

Sister Claudia arched an eyebrow. "It's a pity you don't seem as strong as her. I don't mean no offense by that. I'm merely pointing out an observation. Having Sister Mary as my mentor, I've learned a lot about leadership and the world in which we live. I'm sure you've been learning much the same under your grandmother's mentorship. I'm simply trying to say that it appears you've got plenty more to learn from her."

"Don't worry about me. I'm plenty strong."

"Oh dear, I have offended you. It was just that I've seen the way you defer to your grandmother since being here, and quite frankly, it did not feel like a teacher-student relationship or even a parent-child one. It looked more like a boss and an employee. I feared you may not be getting the proper education you deserved."

Sister Mary let out a soft laugh. "That's enough now. No need to keep teasing the young gal."

Roni did not believe for a second that Sister Mary thought this was playful teasing. But instead of pushing matters, she allowed herself an awkward grin and returned to her food. *Soon,* she thought, *just a few hours and I'll have that book in my possession. Then we'll see who's strong.*

CHAPTER 8

Immediately following the dinner, Roni hastened across the colonnade to the dorm. She stormed down the aisle and knocked on Gram's door. Hearing a choked *Come in* Roni entered to find Gram sitting on the bed with her back against the wall, her legs straight out, her eyes puffy, her nose red.

"Have a seat," Gram said, patting a spot next to her.

"Are you okay? Those nuns had no right to say —"

"It's okay. I've known for a long time the kinds of people they are. Just because they wear the clothes of a nun does not make them nuns. Not in the Catholic sense, anyway."

"I still don't like it."

"I appreciate your loyalty and concern. I've actually been thinking about that a lot tonight — about you. I know you better than you think. That loyalty, that concern — it can be a good thing. You must be careful, though. It can mislead you. It can guide you down the wrong paths."

Roni worried that Gram had been snooping in her room during the dinner. If she found Roni's tomb bag, it would be years before she trusted Roni enough to take her on an outing again.

Blowing her nose into a handkerchief, Gram said, "Do you remember Princess Nanono?"

Roni thought back, the odd name itching under the dark surface of her memories. "Maybe? I'm not sure."

"You were just a little girl. Your mother would make up stories for you. She preferred it over telling you stories like *Three Little Pigs* or *The Boy Who Cried Wolf*. I made sure you learned those stories eventually, but your mother wanted to teach you lessons her own way — everything had to be her own way. Princess Nanono was the star of her storytelling.

"You loved those stories. Each one basically had the Princess getting into some sort of trouble by making the wrong choice, and by the end she would learn her lesson. There were other characters, but I don't really remember them well — a talking cookie, I think, and a bird that was her friend. But the important part here is that you loved the stories and as you started to understand the point of the stories, you became fiercely loyal to Princess Nanono. You worried that she made so many poor decisions. And you started to write your own stories for her — ones in which she was more of a heroine than a victim. Do you recall any of this?"

"A little. I have this vague image of a calico cat — yes, its name was Petal! And sometimes it was bad and sometimes good, so I never knew which version I'd get in a story."

"Good. Then maybe you'll remember this — one morning, you came to breakfast, and you asked your mother where Princess Nanono lived. You wanted to go visit. Because your mother had made these stories up, they were not written down in any book that you would have seen. So, you believed that she was recounting tales of a person she once knew. You wanted to visit her to share your stories so that you might help Princess Nanono. It was that morning in which your mother had to tell you the truth.

"But you refused to believe it. In your mind, there had to be a Princess Nanono. No choice. Otherwise, it meant your mother had lied to you.

"For almost a year after that, you tried everything you could think of to wheedle out information about where the real Princess Nanono lived. None of us would help you because of course none of us had an answer. But you refused to believe us.

"Of course, no matter how much you wished for it, you would never find Princess Nanono. That person never existed." Gram reached over and put her hand atop Roni's. "I know you want to help me. I know you want any chance, no matter how slim, to connect with your mother. But the creature inside that rift is not your mother. It's not the woman who came up with Princess Nanono. Whatever you think is in that rift, no matter how much you wish it to be, it is not your Maria."

"Then it isn't yours either, is it?" The words slipped out of Roni's mouth before she could stop.

Gram rolled her lips in tight and looked away. With the sharp sniffle, she said, "Go to bed. Stop worrying about your mother. Get some sleep."

"Please, Gram, you don't understand —"

"No, you do not understand. I don't expect it, but you need to believe that you will not understand what that thing is. When we get back to Pennsylvania, maybe you'll find something in the library to help. But for now, you must accept that there will always be limits to how much of another universe you can understand. And that includes the creatures within it."

"But if it's even a small portion of your daughter —"

"Enough. Go to your room, get some sleep, and for once, just listen."

Gram's stern face offered no opening for further conversation. Not that Roni wanted it anyway. She stomped off to her room and closed the door hard. Fuming, she thought of the tomb bag. Gram simply did not understand. She had let her emotions get in the way.

Roni wished she could rush over to the library immediately, but she knew she would have to wait. A lot.

Sitting on the edge of the lumpy mattress, Roni listened as the Sisters settled in the dorm for the night. With her jaw clenched and her breathing shallow, she heard every murmured voice, every creaking floorboard, every groan of tired bodies. As the minutes dragged on, the tension in her throat grew worse. She suspected that her voice would be nearly gone by the time she managed to get started on the night's mission — an old nervous habit that hadn't surfaced in about two years.

Good thing I won't have to talk to anybody tonight.

She figured she might not have anybody to talk to for the next several days. Assuming she could complete her mission, none of the nuns would be talking to her and Gram always had enough reasons to play the silent game. Just as well. After the evening's dinner, she had little but angry words to share with any of the people surrounding her at the moment.

Roni stretched back on the bed and closed her eyes. She had earbuds in and connected to her phone. If she managed to fall asleep, her alarm would go off at 3am. By that time, nobody would be awake.

But sleep would not come.

Twice, she considered leaving early — convincing herself that surely everybody had fallen asleep. Near midnight, she even stepped out of her room and walked down to the bathroom. All were asleep except Sister Rachel. She knelt in the middle of her bed and prayed — eyes closed, hands clasped, rosary looped around. If she had noticed Roni, she did not acknowledge the fact. After using the bathroom, Roni returned to her room and attempted once more to get some sleep.

Seconds later, the alarm went off. She startled in bed, a little drool wetting her pillow. Tapping off her phone, she sat up and rubbed her eyes. She figured she had managed at least forty-five minutes of real sleep, maybe even a little over an hour. Better than nothing.

It took her fifteen minutes to fully awaken, check over her tomb bag, and step out into the main room. She kept her shoes in the bag and walked the length of the dorm in her socks. With slow, methodical steps, she inched her way toward the exit. She brought down each step gently, making sure the wood did not creak loud enough to alert any light sleepers.

The room had been split in two. The left side nuns all rattled out hefty snores. The right side slept quietly but some of them rolled or kicked or flapped out a hand.

Reaching the far end, Roni did not breathe relief. Instead, she placed her hand on the doorknob and turned it slowly. Her hands shivered, and she feared the motion might rattle the lock. The next several moments blurred together — finally turning the knob open, pushing the door out, stepping through, keeping the knob open while grabbing it on the other side, closing the door, and easing the knob back. All without making a sound. With that accomplished, she still did not breathe relief. Instead, she scurried across the cold grass until she reached the circle with the statue of the Virgin Mary and the parked rental car.

She lowered to the ground and put on her shoes. Once

finished, she inhaled long and slow and allowed herself a small moment to breathe. Relief.

Roni took another moment to rub her neck, trying to ease some of the tension. But true relaxation would have to wait. She had only accomplished the first part of the evening — getting out of the dorm undetected. Now for the really tough parts.

Hustling across the grass, Roni hoped she moved with the grace of a prowling cat but suspected she clumped along more like a hungry raccoon. Her bag thumped at her side, her feet snapped a twig on the ground, and she tripped at the edge of the concrete path when she reached the library. Only the lateness of the evening saved her from discovery.

Properly humbled, she let her excitement subside so that she could focus on what actually needed to be done. She approached the door to the library like a knight stepping before an ancient ruin — respectful and cautious. In her arsenal, she had a bobby pin and a paperclip. While she lacked experience at picking locks, she understood the basic concept. Starting with a bobby pin in the bottom, she then inserted the paperclip above it, and on the first try, the lock opened. Far too much pride swelled her chest but then deflated as she understood the truth — Sister Ashley had never locked the door in the first place. Roni's picking skills remained pathetic.

An evening shower opened up as she slinked into the library. Though the rain did not hit hard, its gentle tapping against the dorm would help hide any noises she might make. She chuckled — *Perhaps the Lord wants me to get this book.*

She brought up the flashlight app on her phone and headed straight for the stairs leading downward. The late hour made the enclosed space feel tighter, darker. Under the stark, blue light of her phone, the dust and cobwebs created strange shadows and added an unnatural texture to the walls. It was like walking through an old black and white monster movie — which only served Roni an extra heaping of nerves.

She sped through the passageways, spying several of her marks in the dust to aid her in making the proper turns. At least, she thought so. Until she reached a dead end.

Tracing back her steps, she inspected the dust mark closer. Which direction did it indicate? Was it even her sign or did something else brush across the corner? Perhaps her fingermarks could have been clearer. She chose a different path which also ended up dead. Back again, and again, and again.

After several attempts, she walked upon her starting point — the staircase. Murmuring swears, she began over in hopes of finding where she had gone wrong. A full hour went by.

Roni's pace quickened as she scuttled through the passageways once more. Sweat beaded along her back even as her mouth dried with the dust of the dead.

At another intersection which looked both familiar and foreign, she stopped. Pinching the bridge of her nose, she let out a frustrated groan. This could not be happening.

Then she heard a sound that changed everything — *Woooooooo.*

Roni held her breath so she could distinguish the sound clearly. *Wooooooo.* Definitely the same cry of wind going through a poorly made bagpipe.

After a few breaths, she stopped again to listen. To her right. She headed down that path until she reached the next junction. Then she held her breath and listened. *Wooooo.* Straight, this time.

Twice more she had to stop and use that horrible sound

as her guide. In less than five minutes, she came upon the big door with the iron ring for a knob. The door stood ajar as if inviting her entrance — Sister Ashley must have forgotten to lock the door in her haste to reach dinner. Roni would be sure to leave it open later to avoid tipping the nuns off. Patting her bag, making sure she still held all of the things she had brought along, she entered the private study of Sister Agnes.

Everything appeared as it had during her first visit — which meant Sister Ashley had returned at some point after dinner to straighten up. Roni wondered if the young gal wanted to follow in the footsteps of Sister Agnes. Perhaps she truly intended to live down here one day — sequestered with only the books around her.

The room felt smaller than before as if it wanted to lean in and watch everything Roni planned. *Well then, watch this,* she thought, getting straight to work. She set the bag down next to the desk and positioned herself at the foot of the bed. Bending at the knees, she gripped the heavy wooden frame and lifted. It had been heavy enough with the help of Sister Ashley, but alone, Roni budged the thing only two inches. She repeated the motion — moving the bed two inches at a time.

After she had managed close to a foot, she stopped to catch her breath. She slumped onto the bed and stuck her arm toward the crevice Sister Agnes rested in. Not enough room yet.

Ignoring the dampness of her shirt against her back, Roni lugged the bed three more times. While this did not make getting the book as easy as earlier in the day, she did manage enough space that she could spider her fingers around the book's spine. The hard surface rubbing the back of her fingers had to be the bones of Sister Agnes — Roni closed her eyes and tried to wash away any image that thought dared to conjure.

Despite the awkward angle, she managed to pull the book free. With a soft yip, she dropped onto the floor and hugged the large volume to her chest — breathing hard, sweating, and hoping she had not disturbed Sister Agnes too greatly. The nuns would be mad at her for stealing the book. They would be furious if she had damaged Sister Agnes.

Holding the book, feeling its energy pulse against her chest, Roni posed a simple question — *what next?* Her plan had been clear enough. She wanted to take the book back to Pennsylvania. After her research had proved fruitless for finding a way to save Maria, she at least could return this book to the caverns.

No. She could not start lying to herself now. Not after she had made it this far. She had done this for one reason only — to save Maria. No. Full honesty. To save Maria, her mother. The only reason this particular book could have been secreted all the way down here instead of returned to the caverns was that it held value connected with the rift.

The real question was not *what now?* But rather *what exactly is the nature of the universe contained in the book?*

"Only one way to find out," Roni muttered to the empty room.

She clambered to her feet and held the book at arm's length. Experience had taught her how dangerous a book like this could be, so she had to be careful how she went about opening it. A quick scan of the room confirmed her suspicions — the old bed frame was the heaviest object.

Roni lifted the stained mattress and looked at the rope lattice underneath. It might work.

Taking out her journal and pen, she sat at the desk and wrote a quick entry describing the events that had led up to this point. If things went badly, she wanted some record of what had happened. At length, she returned the journal and pen to her bag and set them aside.

Next, she moved the desk chair so that its back pressed up against the bed frame and that it faced the door. Roni stepped over the frame, putting one leg between the gaps in the rope. She then lowered herself to her knees. With the chair in front of her, she propped the book up against its back.

All she had to do was reach around to the front of the chair and open the book. Whatever came out of it or went into it would be facing the direction of the door — not her. If she lost control of the book and the room depressurized, she hoped the weight of the bed would anchor her to this universe. The distant voice of a long-forgotten science teacher reminded her that any system was only as strong as its weakest point.

She yanked hard on the ropes. Though they held, she thought they surely would be the first thing to snap. But everything in the room was old and brittle except the hardwoods. She would just have to make do.

She reached for the book. But stopped.

Moving fast, so as not to lose her will, she unfastened her belt and looped it around the side runner of the bed. She slipped her arm through the loop and tightened it as far as it would go. Between that and the rope and the bed frame itself, if she fell into the book's universe, she suspected her limbs would stay behind.

Blotting that image from her mind, she used her free arm to stretch out and pull the front cover open.

The book cover resisted. That suggested a different pressure level inside that book's universe — one that would suck all the air from the room until the pressure equalized. Either that or the old book had not been opened in ages and might simply be sticking. Reworking her grip, Roni took a deep breath and readied to pull harder on the cover.

The study door opened and Sister Claudia entered with Sister Ashley by her side. They took one look at the book and screamed.

Roni jolted, her heart jackhammering against her chest. As she disentangled from the bed, Sister Claudia entered and immediately sidestepped out of direct line of sight of the book. Sister Ashley followed to the opposite side.

"Are you okay? I'm sorry that I came down here without you," Roni said. "I know you think this book is part of your history, with Sister Agnes and all, calling it the *History of Secrets*. But that's not true. It's one of the Parallel Society's books and it can cause you great harm. I'm trying to help."

Sister Claudia clasped her hands behind her back. "Do not make matters worse by lying to us. We did not scream because we thought you had betrayed us. We did not scream out of fear."

"A little fear," Sister Ashley said. "I did not want to be in front of that book."

"We were taken by surprise. That's all. And now that we see what you've done, we know you have to ability to change things for us."

Roni settled on the edge of the wood frame. She frowned. "I do?"

Sister Ashley knelt next to Roni. "This is going to be a glorious day. We finally have somebody willing to touch the book and able, too. We finally have somebody who can help us."

"I'm going to help you?"

"Oh, indeed," Sister Claudia said, her eyes darkening as she lowered her head. "You're going to do exactly what I tell you."

CHAPTER 9

Sister Ashley set two flashlights face up toward the ceiling to fully light the room while Sister Claudia paced a small circle, never taking her eyes off Roni. The book remained closed on the desk chair. Wind continued to blow above filling the room with more of that awful whining.

Sister Claudia stopped and gazed down upon Roni. Her habit blended in with the murky surroundings turning her into a ghostly, floating figure. "I'm afraid Sister Mary will be quite angry, if she discovers what you've done."

Roni choked down all the sarcastic comments that crept up her throat. A sharp bite rushed back. "Perhaps you were not listening when you came in here and boasted how you weren't frightened. The fact remains that this book does not belong to you."

"Your arrogance is annoying. A little impressive but mostly annoying."

Sister Ashley stepped forward and with a respectful bow, she said, "Let us not lose sight of our purpose here."

Sister Claudia glowered at Sister Ashley for a stretched second or two. Long enough to cause Sister Ashley visible discomfort. Only then did Sister Claudia gesture to the book and Roni. "Will you please move that book aside?"

As if removing a weapon, Roni lifted the book and set it on the floor. Sister Claudia slid the chair around so that she could sit facing Roni. "I'm going to give you a choice. It is my sincere hope that once you understand the true context of the situation that you will choose to help us."

"I have a choice now? I thought I had to do what you wanted."

Sister Ashley stepped up from behind. "With the book we can actually control the conduit."

With a sharp swat of her hand, Sister Claudia caught Sister Ashley on the chin. "Be quiet."

"What is she talking about?" Roni asked. Her stomach flipped as her mind raced to catch up with the shifting moods in the room.

Sister Claudia pressed her hands upon her knees. Her fingers dug in like claws. "As I was trying to say, you need context in order to make your decision. Be a good student, keep your mouth shut and listen." She glanced over her shoulder. "Both of you."

Sister Ashley bowed again and stepped back toward the wall. "Ay."

After a short breath to compose herself, Sister Claudia said, "This abbey has stood since the 1600s. Sisters Margaret and Agnes lived here together in the early 1800s — beginning in 1804. Margaret and Agnes were more than Sisters of the Abbey, they were actual sisters, too. Their father farmed for a time but eventually found drink to be more appealing. The mother worked hard to maintain the family. Died when the girls were young. They came to the Abbey in their early teens. More than anything, I believe that fact caused too much of the troubles between them.

"Like any siblings, they competed with each other. Even in their duties that were meant to be benevolent and giving.

If Margaret sacrificed a day to help the poor, Agnes would devote a week. If Agnes spent two hours in devotional prayer, the next night Margaret would spend three. According to some of the records Sister Ashley has uncovered, this rivalry was seen by the other nuns as a healthy situation." Turning her head aside, Sister Claudia said, "Isn't that right?"

Sister Ashley took one step forward. "Ay, it is. Sister Anne, the head of the Abbey at the time, believed that the competition would bring out the best, most altruistic behavior by the sisters, and in doing so, that they would end up being models for the other nuns to follow."

"The church may move slowly when it comes to change, but at least I can say that were the two sisters in the Abbey today, they would not be pitted against each other. But the 1800s was a different time with different views.

"Now, I am not clear on how much your grandmother has shared with you about our history, but you should know that our conduit to Heaven opened several hundred years ago. For Sisters Margaret and Agnes, just like it is for me and Sister Ashley, the conduit always was. Which brings me to the last part necessary to understanding all of this — and that part is our book on the floor."

Roni's foot slid against the book's spine.

If Sister Claudia noticed, she did not acknowledge it. "According to Sister Ashley's research, Sister Anne was the first to reach out to the Parallel Society."

"That's right," Sister Ashley said, unable to see Sister Claudia's scowl. "It's unclear how Sister Anne discovered the existence of the Society, but she wrote a letter to them and within a few months, they sent their first representatives here."

"The Society member, a woman named Caroline Grosvenor, brought that book with her. She explained that the book could be used to contain our conduit and that the Society would dispose of it later. Well, I'm sure you understand by now that we were not in favor of that approach. Sister Anne made it quite clear in her letter that we wanted to secure the conduit to protect those around it and to safely examine it. We were thrilled to have this connection to Heaven — and still are — but at the time, it had managed to injure several of the nuns and engulf two more. We are not foolish enough to think that they were brought to Heaven. It is clear from the scrolls of Sister Anne and Sister Margaret that those unfortunate souls died before they fully entered the conduit. They wanted the Society to use its specialized knowledge to help the nuns communicate with Heaven, and to do that, we needed the conduit to be stable and secure. That's all they wanted. But, of course, Ms. Grosvenor did not see it that way.

"The Lord, however, controls all and sees all. So, when Ms. Grosvenor knew we would not help her destroy the conduit, she contacted the Irish government. That did not go as she had planned. They arrived and heard what we had to say and saw what we had to show, and it was agreed that we could not risk closing this conduit. If the nuns were right and the Irish government went ahead as the Society wanted, then they would be responsible for destroying what could become a national treasure. They saw money flowing in from all those who wanted to touch Heaven. If the nuns were wrong, then surely the Society could fix matters as needed at a later date.

"Ms. Grosvenor was quite angry, but she had no power in the situation. So, with the help of Sister Anne and Sister Margaret, it was finally agreed to create the stabilizing set up we have today. In exchange, the Abbey agreed to keep the existence of the conduit private. That suited us fine. We recognized then and now that the world is not ready for such a revelation. Our sacred duty is to protect this conduit from all who would harm it, which sadly means protecting it from the majority of the world. Everything else you've heard about us or the conduit is nothing more than fabrications created by your Society."

Roni did not know how much of this to believe but found the idea that Gram had lied to her about the rift plausible. "I'm guessing this is where Sister Agnes comes in?"

"She was not about to let her sister and some woman from some Society take away the beautiful things she had experienced. At least, that is how many see it now. Other nuns in the past have suggested that it was more sibling rivalry, more pushing for power, and all other sorts of corrupt or impure approaches. But those of us who've done the research know the truth. And those of us who've seen an angel firsthand — well, we really know. It is the same *before and after* affect that you have experienced. You know it. Once you've witnessed such a thing, it forever changes you. And Sister Agnes was no different. If anything, the oddity in all of this was with Sister Margaret. How she could open the church doors to a stranger, how she could make deals with the government, instead of letting the glory of Heaven spread throughout the world — I've never understood it."

Once more, Sister Ashley stepped forward. Sister Claudia raised a hand, ready to strike. Sister Ashley backed away.

"The evening before Ms. Grosvenor left the Abbey, Sister Agnes did much like you this evening — she snuck around the dorms while everyone slept, and she swiped this incredible book from underneath Ms. Grosvenor's bed. She stole away down here — Sister Ashley tells me that this room existed long before Sister Agnes — and she made it her home."

A glance back prompted Sister Ashley to move closer. "That is correct. In that the tomb was built with this room — an unusual construction for the unusual job of tomb-keeper. I've never found another reference in an Abbey to such a position, but this Abbey has never been like others anyway."

"From here, Sister Agnes wrote her thoughts, protected the book, and led those nuns willing to follow her. Aboveground, Sister Margaret took over as Head of the Abbey, and all the sisters did her bidding. But the followers of Sister Agnes also carried out orders from below. And it remained that way until their deaths." Glancing up at Sister Ashley, Sister Claudia added, "Tell her about the vow."

Sister Ashley hesitated, her focus entirely on Sister Claudia. She nodded, opened her mouth, but flinched back.

"Well?" Sister Claudia snapped.

With an uneasy grin, Sister Ashley cleared her throat. "You have to understand that Sister Margaret and Sister Agnes knew of each other's positions. It was not like a secret spy network or something like that. Sister Margaret tolerated Sister Agnes because of the vow. It was a simple agreement — that no nun would ever touch the book. Sister Margaret, of course, wanted everyone to make the vow so that she knew her deals with the Parallel Society and the Irish government would not be broken."

"But Sister Agnes," Roni said. "Why would she agree?"

"That is quite clear. You see, Sister Agnes opened the book. Once. It did not take her life, but what she witnessed made her believe that the power inside of it should not be wielded by any nun. Possibly not by anybody in the world at all, but we can only trust ourselves to honor the vow. So that is what they did, and that is what we do.

"Since that time, Sister Margaret's side of things

concluded that the book itself had created the conduit."

Sister Ashley added, "Which is why Sister Petra's scrolls point out that only the book can reclaim it. She followed Sister Margaret and thought that —"

"Enough." Sister Claudia closed her eyes, wincing as if suffering the pain of a cracked tooth. "You'll have to excuse the Sister. Her excitement is getting the better of her manners."

"You've got it wrong," Roni said. "These books are dangerous."

"Which is why we don't touch them."

"I thought you didn't touch them because of the vow."

"And that vow came partly out of respecting the danger inherent in those books. But you have the experience that we lack. Is that not what the Parallel Society is all about? Learning how to deal with these books and what they can do?"

Staying out of Sister Claudia's reach, Sister Ashley said, "I've read all that Sister Agnes ever wrote. Most of Sister Petra's work, too. That book can do what no other book can do. With the conduit held in place by the other Society books, the one you have found can pull the Angel free."

Roni rose, but Sister Claudia did not back out of the way. With their knees brushing, Roni said, "You think you can pull an angel out of that rift?"

Though Sister Claudia had to look up, she still maintained dominant strength from her position. "No. We think *you* can. You have no vow holding you back from touching the book. And isn't it what you want? To pull out the girl you saw in the conduit?"

The next few seconds might as well have been hours. Roni's head rifled through thoughts that tumbled and spun upon each other with parts of each idea being called out and spread into other ideas. In one instant, she saw the eager and open face of Sister Ashley. The young nun clearly loved her books and had an obsession with the work of Sister Agnes. Perhaps part of her truly wanted to help Roni — even if a self-interested part wanted to free what she thought to be an angel. However, in that same instant, Roni saw salivating, sharp-teethed creatures dressed as nuns. Gram had said they were dangerous, and Roni wondered if this sudden shift was more than simply self-interest but carried with it a darkness that might create a shadow over her.

After all, a year ago, her father had warned her that her actions with the Parallel Society were doing great harm. What if moments like this were the kind of things he referred to?

In the next second, Roni decided it didn't matter. She had never trusted the nuns from the start, so she would not do so now. But that did not mean she forbade herself from using the nuns. One thing was clear — this book possibly held within it the power to free whatever remained of Roni's mother. Once she had Maria out of the rift, then the nuns could think of it as a conduit to Heaven for the rest of eternity. It did not matter to Roni. She would happily visit every year to keep the rift stable. As long as she had Maria, the rest didn't matter.

But in that same second, she thought of Gram. Despite their acrimony, Roni loved her grandmother. She understood how much pain this caused Gram. Coming to the Abbey, year after year, seeing an echo of her daughter trapped in another universe — no, Roni would not be so arrogant as to think she understood. In truth, nobody understood. How could anyone? Gram endured the torture of her loss alone. No other woman in all of history could have experienced what Gram had suffered. It wasn't simply the loss of her daughter. It was seeing her lost daughter both alive and dead, a split existence, never to be made whole again.

One more second ticked by. Roni's instincts conflicted within her. She wanted to save Maria. She wanted to respect Gram. She wanted to fix a wrong from long ago. She did not trust the nuns.

Sister Claudia and Sister Ashley stared at her — expectant, hungry. Roni opened her mouth, ready to tell the nuns in a crude manner that they could screw off, but a voice stopped her. A soft, high-pitched voice. It called to her. The voice of a young girl. Trapped. It sounded like an out of tune flute.

Time sped back to its normal pace. Roni glanced up at the ceiling and heard the wind blowing through the ventilation once more. The corners of her mouth lifted. The world above, Sister Margaret's world, had always been connected with the world below, that of Sister Agnes. Connected but separate. Like two universes, each staying where it belonged.

"Maria does not belong in that rift. If you're speaking the truth, then I am obligated to take this book and pull her out. I am a member of the Parallel Society, and it is my sworn duty to keep universes from crashing into each other." Roni bent down and picked up the book.

"Wonderful," Sister Ashley said, rushing towards Roni with her arms open wide.

Roni inched to the side. "Careful. You don't want to accidentally touch the book."

Sister Ashley pulled her hands back as if threatened by a rattlesnake. "You're correct about that. Thank you for helping us. Not only are you doing the nuns a great service and helping yourself, you save us the trouble of having to bring charges against you for desecrating our tombs."

Sister Claudia snapped her fingers. "Enough chatting.

Let's get this done. Come."

Before Roni could ask Sister Ashley to elaborate, the nuns exited the room, leaving Roni with the choice to follow or find her way out by herself. She followed.

As they wound their way back into the library, across the colonnade, into the church, and down the spiral staircase toward the rift, Roni fought the urge to doubt her decision. The gulf between knowing that the nuns could not be trusted and her desire to save Maria continued to widen, but she saw no easy fix. Stepping in front of the rift told her time was up. Instead, she focused her mind on how to help Maria. A lot of that would depend on what happened when she opened the book.

The rift crackled like a campfire. Its bright red and orange swirls radiated light and heat upon the room. Roni's muscles clenched and she stuttered a step. For a brief instant, she wished Gram were by her side.

But no — she could do this herself. She had to. After all, what kind of leader would she be, if she could not help her own mother?

Sister Claudia and Sister Ashley formed a rough circle with Roni. They bowed their heads. Sister Claudia genuflected and said, "Before we embark on this vital moment, let us pray."

Sister Ashley bowed her head a little more. Out of respect, Roni lowered her head. She watched Sister Ashley — her meekness, her strengths, her enthusiasm, even her subservience fit her perfectly. Her habit and coif, though — while covering her in the most utilitarian way — still managed to express some of her feminine form. Yet at the same time, Roni noticed the light circles of sweat stains on the white of her wimple.

Sister Claudia raised her head with her eyes closed. "Oh Lord, we seek your blessing and your sturdy hand as we set forth to do your work."

Having no use for prayers, Roni closed her eyes and conjured the images of Gram, Sully, and Elliot. That elderly trio had saved more lives than they could ever be thanked for. They made tough decisions, too. Sometimes, they even made decisions they knew would make the others angry. But saving people was what they did.

The things Roni had seen in the last two years, the world that had been opened up to her, even the arguments and frustrations — she saw how it all led to this moment. Ever since joining the Parallel Society, she had been waiting for some ceremony or ID card or secret handshake — something to signify that she truly belonged there, that she had earned her right to be there. But it was never something they could give her. It was something she had to take for herself by doing the very thing they were tasked to do. Not only would she soon save Maria, but she would soon prove that she had the right to call herself one of the Parallel Society.

"In the Lord's name, Amen." Sister Claudia stood and faced the rift. She gestured toward Roni as if nudging a child toward the edge of the deep end of the pool.

Time to sink or swim.

Roni walked forward until she could no longer see the nuns. Better that they were behind her. Light flashed off the rift as if it knew she meant it harm. Readjusting the book in her grip, she also set her right foot back and out, forming a sturdy stance to help her withstand the expected forces.

"Is there a problem?" Sister Claudia asked, her voice cold and threatening.

"Be quiet," Roni said, keeping her focus on the rift. "You've done your part. Leave this to an expert."

Narrowing her eyes, she opened the book.

CHAPTER 10

As Roni pulled open the book cover, grey smoke puffed out. But nothing followed. Dust figured to be the culprit and not some ancient mist from an unknown universe. Then the book vibrated in her hand — gently like a humming refrigerator.

She felt slight pressure upon her palms as if the book pushed against her. Or something pushed against the book in her direction. The longer it lasted, the more she equated the sensation with holding a magnet against another of equal polarity. That was it, exactly. The universe of the book and the universe in the church pushed against each other.

Her heart sank. "This won't work. This is the wrong book."

"Have faith," Sister Claudia said. "It will work."

Roni remained standing still with the book open. But its large size grew heavy in her hands. "I'm telling you, this is the wrong book. We don't want one that's pushing against the rift universe. We want one that extracts from it. Did Sister Agnes steal a different book from the Society as well?"

Despite wanting to close the cover, Roni kept it open and watched the universe in front of her. Much of the orange had slipped away, leaving behind deep crimson. Dark, smoky clouds spun by like miniature storms seen from above. It gave the rift a sense of motion as if it spun on a slow-moving pedestal.

And then Roni saw it. Crawling into view. The young girl. Maria.

As she came closer to facing them full-on, the book reacted. A blast of gold energy whipped out like a frog's tongue. Thin and long, it stretched straight to the rift. Its golden light filled the room, devouring the shadows, leaving every cracked stone and split timber visible.

"You see it now," Sister Ashley said dropping to her knees. "This is the book that created the conduit with its golden light of Heaven."

This tongue of energy had penetrated the rift and wrapped around Maria's arm. It reeled back into the book, strong and taut, pulling on Maria. In seconds, the little girl ended up hovering in the middle of the church basement, locked between two universes. The rift bulged out with her, determined to hold on. The golden tongue freed her arm and pulled harder.

Sister Claudia put out her hands. "She's beautiful. A true angel."

Crackling sparks and bulging waves rolled along the surface of the rift. The circle of books pushed all the rift's energy back in onto itself. Except for Maria. The books could not contain her. By the time Maria floated equidistant between Roni's open book and the rift, her head tore free from the rift's grasp. Even as the rest of her body remained wrapped in a menacing red blob of power, even as the golden tongue strained to pull her, even as her mouth opened wide and cried in pain — through all of it, she had the ability to lock eyes with Roni.

A fleeting second. No more. But enough to erase all doubt from Roni. This was her mother as a child. Gram's daughter. All that remained.

From behind, Roni heard Sister Ashley ask, "Now?"

For one beat of her heart, Roni heard the betrayal in that voice. She did not know what it meant, but she knew it would be bad.

"Oh, yes," Sister Claudia said. "Definitely now."

With an ecstatic squeal, Sister Ashley sprinted forward. Roni could only watch. Any effort to stop Sister Ashley meant losing control of the book — and losing Maria. Sister Claudia's gleeful laugh erupted behind.

"Sister Agnes understood what all the nuns before her failed to understand," Sister Claudia said as Sister Ashley danced around the circle of books. "This is more than simply a conduit, more than simply a way to communicate with angels in Heaven. This is a gateway to Heaven itself. Keeping this locked away, encircled by your books, is a heresy."

Over her shoulder Roni yelled, "Don't do this. Whatever you're planning, just don't." Turning her focus back to Maria, she went on, "Fight. You're running out of time. Come to me."

"She won't have to fight. None of us will."

Sister Ashley whipped off her wimple and coif, letting long locks of raven hair flow around her shoulders.

Mesmerized, Sister Claudia went on, "For centuries scholars have debated how we would know when Jesus had returned. How would we know that the time had come to create Heaven on Earth? And all that time, the nuns here at the Abbey already held the answer."

"Jesus was never going to be seen in mortal form," Sister Ashley said, her voice in a trance. "Sister Agnes knew t all along. Jesus brought us the conduit, and it is ourr and duty to bring Heaven onto the Earth."

She moved like a ballerina, and as she finished her words
she bent forward and gently lifted one of the Society books
out of the circle. A ripple in the air soared around the
remaining books. Roni's heart sank.

And Hell broke loose.

"No," Roni said, her white-knuckled fingers trembling.

In her delirious exultation's, Sister Ashley twirled as she
held the book out. The rift flashed red light like an angry
storm. Its edges undulated, including those surrounding
Maria.

"Help," Maria said, her voice strained, her eyes tearing.

Sister Ashley froze in an awkward stance as she stared at
Maria. "Yes, my Lord. I can help. I can free you from this
pain." With a jerking motion, she threw the book into the
nearest group of bookstands. Two more knocked over.

Vicious winds arose as if a tornado had formed within
the room. The books still operating shuttered in their
stands. Sister Ashley laughed as the wind thrust her hair
wildly around. Roni tried to scoot back, hoping her efforts
might spool the tongue in quicker or at least bring Maria
further from the rift. But the icy hand of Sister Claudia
touched her shoulder.

"That won't work."

All of the bookstands lifted off the ground. The books
flew about. A bolt of lightning broke free from the rift and
carved a hole into the stone wall. Howls and moans and
twisted cries filled the room as if the stones themselves
screamed.

Roni repositioned her hands, but there was no way to
hold the oversized book with one hand and attempt to grab
Maria with the other. The book required both her hands to
stay open, and she could not close it without giving up on

her mother. She refused.

Two metal stands clattered in one corner while a wooden stand shattered against another. Sister Ashley giggled at the orchestration of noise. She looked back at Sister Claudia. "It's really happening. Isn't it wonderful?"

A large stone book stand flew through the air and clobbered Sister Ashley in the side. She tumbled to the ground, her head banging against the hard floor. Blood splashed across the stones.

Wobbling on all fours, she attempted to stand. The strong winds and the blow to her head shoved her back down. With both hands supporting her, Sister Ashley gazed about the room. Blood dribbled from under her hair, across her forehead, and down her cheeks.

She uttered a confused gasp.

With a sharp crack in the air, the orange rift shot out a lance of energy, took hold of Sister Ashley, and yanked her inside.

Two seconds, and she was gone.

The open books shot off energy in all directions. They bounced around like bumper cars. One flew off near Roni's head and another smacked into her shins.

Amongst the chaos, Sister Claudia crossed herself. She stared at the empty spot where Sister Ashley had been. "Incredible."

"The books," Roni said. "Close the books and put them back in place."

As if speaking to a thick child, Sister Claudia said, "You don't close Heaven."

Roni gave one last glance at Sister Claudia. No help would be coming from there. She faced her mother again. "Maria, come on. Fight. You can break free."

She could not tell if Maria heard her or even understood her, but the young girl stretched her arms further towards

Roni. She wriggled as if pushing through a tight space. Her face stretched back and she winced.

Another book, this one spinning like a pinwheel, cut through the air and clipped Sister Claudia on the chin. She only smiled — even as the blood slid down her throat and stained her gown. "Creation is always violent. I understand that, my Lord. I am ready. If you must take my life as you have taken Sister Ashley, I am yours." She ambled forward, a psychotic grin plastered across her lips.

In the distance, Roni heard a rumble and had the strange thought that a thunderstorm might be brewing outside. But the rumble quickly intensified. Rolling closer and closer. It became a stampede thundering down upon them.

The rift burst open.

A red wave jetted out in all directions. When it struck Roni, it lifted her off the floor and tumbled her backwards. The book flew from her hands, and as it rose, time slowed.

Not just a perceptional slowing. Time actually slowed.

She floated in the air, feeling the pull of gravity combating the push of the wave. She felt the air shoving out of her lungs. Her hair thrust back as the room tilted in front of her. But it all moved glacially.

In fact, Roni felt the slowing down more and more each passing moment — she dared not think of it as seconds. And then everything stopped. Locked in the air, unable to move, frozen in place. Yet she could still feel life around her. And with an intuitive leap, she put it together — the world inside this universe moved, but so imperceptibly slow as to be frozen in time. All the years that had passed since part of Maria had split off into the rift, yet for that part of her, perhaps only a few seconds had gone by. A minute at most. Even sound moved so slowly that Roni heard the purist silence ever in her life.

Yet her thoughts kept moving. Which suggested Maria's

thoughts had continued all this time as well. How many years had gone before she realized what was happening to her? How many years did she strain and struggle with the misguided hope that she could break free? How long before she gave up?

A distant rumble struck Roni's ears — notable not only because it stood out amongst the silence but also because it sounded in real time, not slowed down. It sounded like a stampede of wild mustangs. The closer it came, the more the sound rendered into a steady thrum. She could feel it vibrating her bones, her skin, even the hairs growing on her arms.

When the thrum hit, the speed of the world returned to normal. Roni's body flipped through the air and slammed onto the hard floor. Sister Claudia shot backwards, smacking into the wall, and crashing on her hands and knees. The open books fell — several of them flapping shut, several others apparently inert. But not the big book Roni had opened.

It lay flat on the floor about ten feet away. Its strange gold light poured out, creating twisted shadows on the ceiling as it fought to engulf Maria. The young girl screamed. She braced her hands against the floor. From the waist down, she was inside the book. Tears streamed off her chin.

Roni snatched a look at the rift. Its swirling storms had settled and its deep vibrant colors had dimmed. Ignoring the throbs of pain radiating from her bones, she raced across the room and clutched both of Maria's hands. Straddling the book, Roni arched back, pulling, pulling, groaning in an effort to find a little more strength.

"Sister Claudia," she called out as she repositioned her feet. Across the room she saw the nun praying on her knees. "Get over here. Help me save this girl."

But Sister Claudia shook her head. "It wasn't supposed to be like this. I don't understand."

Sweat covered Roni's body. Her grip on Maria slipped a few inches. She looked down as the little girl stared directly into her. No mistaking those eyes — they pleaded for her life.

The gold tongue slithered around Maria, settling across her chest and on her shoulder. It constricted as it pulled her further down. Roni dropped to her knees, still clutching Maria, still pulling back, feeling her muscles strain and tear. Feeling all of her strength weaken.

"Sister Claudia. Please."

Sister Claudia stood, and through a glimmer of hope, Roni thought all would be well. But the glimmer faded as the nun bolted for the spiral staircase leading upward.

At the foot of the staircase, she halted. She stumbled backwards, her face agape. Sister Mary descended the stairs and behind her came Gram, Sully, and Elliot. All four paused to survey the situation.

Hunched over and pushing his glasses up his nose, Sully set his feet firm on the floor. "Gram, take care of those books." Gram moved around Sully and flicked her wrists. Long chains fell from the sleeves of her blouse. Like a seasoned cowboy, she whipped those chains across the room. Each one found its mark — the spine of a book. She hauled them in, tied them up, and set about placing them on the bookstands.

Sister Mary snapped her fingers at Sister Claudia and the two helped Gram reset the bookstands.

"Elliot," Sully said and his old partner needed no more.

The tall, distinguished man headed over to Sister Claudia. If she had suffered any wounds, he would heal her.

Finally, Sully approached Roni. He reached down, and with an iron grip, he grabbed Roni by the waist. She had seen his gifts in action before. Like a boulder, he could be immovable. And though she spotted the anger in his face, she felt relief at the arrival of the Parallel Society.

Until the heavy bowling sound returned. Rolling, rolling. Turning into a stampede of wild mustangs.

Roni's eyes snapped wide open. "Get out of the — "

The red wave hit harder than before. It blasted Roni off her feet, but with Sully holding her, her body twisted over his shoulder. Her ribs snapped like a chain of firecrackers. It was the last sound she heard before the wave stole all sound.

Immobilized and contorted, Roni suffered through her cracked rib cage in an unending loop of pain. An agonized shriek rose in her chest but could not escape. In this red universe, it would take decades for her mouth to open wide enough to release the sound.

From the corner of her eye, she snatched a glimpse of the book. The upside-down image promised to haunt her for the rest of her life. It remained on the floor, open, and all trace of Maria had vanished.

Roni tried to scan the area, but with her head tucked under and motionless, her limited view provided nothing more. When she finally heard the distant rumble, relief blended with terror in her heart. The wave would pass soon but the pain would only amplify.

As the rumble approached and the volume grew louder, Roni mentally braced herself. And then it was upon them. The stampede plowed across them as the wave finished its course.

The world returned to normal. Roni's legs continued to spin overhead, twisting her body, and the electrifying jolts in her chest pressed down like knives into her lungs. She screamed out, and as her body slipped from Sully's grip, she had an instant in which she saw Gram, Sister Mary, Sister

Claudia, and Elliot flailing through the air. Sully arched back and watched her in confusion.

She hit the floor head first. Purple-black dots flashed across her vision.

All went dark.

CHAPTER 11

Roni's eyes fluttered open. She lay in the lumpy guest bed of the nuns' dorm. A tall, black man stood over her. He held a gnarled cane parallel to her body in his right hand while his left hand prescribed a series of motions in the air. *Elliot.*

She grinned, then chuckled. "Did you save my life again?"

"Be quiet," he said with his deep, precise voice. "You are well, but you should take it easy for the rest of the day."

Propping up on her elbows, she winced at the soreness. Better the sensation of bruising rather than the hot piercing of broken ribs cutting her apart from the inside.

Elliot snapped his fingers at her. "I told you to take it easy and the first thing you do is try to sit up. You are as stubborn as your grandmother."

"I can't let some broken bones stop me right now."

"You had a collapsed lung, too."

"I did?"

From the doorway, Sully stood with his arms crossed. "Probably a concussion, on top of that. But by all means, ignore Elliot and go get yourself hurt again."

Roni pushed herself to a fully upright position. Elliot huffed, but he stepped back and leaned on his cane. Sully's head made a slow scan as he took in the meager private room.

"Maybe we should leave you here," he said. "Perhaps a year or two stuck in the Abbey might straighten you out."

"You're not the first to suggest that one."

"I wonder why that might be?"

Roni's face wrinkled tight. "You think I wanted any of this to happen?"

"I think you lack the common decency to respect those who stick their necks out for you. Your grandmother did not want you to go on this trip. She said you weren't ready. I vouched for you. I used up some of my capital as a leader so that you would be sent on this trip. And look what you did."

As all of the events flooded back to her, Roni turned her apprehensive eyes upon Elliot. He put out a reassuring hand. "Everybody is okay," he said. "The rift is not stabilized, but we were able to create a temporary method of controlling it."

"Temporary, at best," Sully said. "Do you have any idea how difficult that was? I had to use more of my strength than I've done in years just to keep those pedestals in place. Elliot worked a shield to keep the building from collapsing upon us. And your dear Gram worked tirelessly to chain together what little we could. Many of the books were damaged. Some beyond our ability to repair from here. Some might never be useable again."

Pressing his hand harder in comfort, Elliot said, "Once we have the full complement of books repaired or created, all will be well. Until then, the rift will have to be carefully monitored."

"And Gram?" Roni asked.

"She is fine."

With a disgusted snort, Sully said, "She is far from fine. Poor woman has had to lose her daughter for a second time."

Roni's eyes welled up. "Then ... Maria's gone?"

"I'm afraid so," Elliot said, his brow wrinkling into numerous folds.

"Maria died years ago in a car accident," Sully said. He gritted his teeth tight enough to turn his jaw as white as the tufts of hair ringing his bald head. "That thing in the rift was no more than a memory of Gram's daughter. And it was never your mother. You get that straight. That little afterimage of a girl never grew up to be an adult, never fell in love, never got married, never spent an intimate night creating you, never gave birth to you, never —"

"I get it. You don't have to be a prick about it."

"Looking at the mess around here, I think I do."

Elliot sliced his hand through the air between Roni and Sully. "That is quite enough from both of you."

Plunking her elbows onto her knees, Roni lowered her head into her hands. Fighting with Sully would not solve anything. It certainly would not bring back Maria. Roni had been so close, had the girl in her arms, but now — Maria was most likely lost in another universe. Again.

Roni's head perked up at a soft high-pitched sound. The soft mewing of a cat. Faint and distant. Why would she hear that? She could not recall having seen any cats or evidence of cats around the Abbey property. And she was fairly certain it would be difficult for a cat to wander onto the property — being so far from any other homes or towns.

It came again. "Did you hear that?"

"Hear what?" Elliot asked.

"Sully?"

"I only hear you making excuses for your bad behavior."

"Do not start again," Elliot said. He stepped closer to Sully and lowered his head to speak softly — though Roni could hear them quite clearly. "It is evident that she feels bad enough about what has happened. You've done your job in reprimanding her and asserting your authority. There is no need to keep opening the wound."

Sully did not look convinced. "Until that rift is stabilized, things are not okay here. And until we can figure out what Sister Ashley's presence within the rift will do, we have no idea if that stability is even possible. Because let's face it — that universe is not like some mass expanse of space with planets and stars. At least, that's not the sense I've got from it. It acts more like a living being of its own."

Roni got to her feet. "Maria is not in the rift anymore, but she fell in that book. Shouldn't we go get her?"

"One crisis at a time," Sully said.

"But it'd be easy. We could do what we did with Darin. You build a golem, have it go in there, and bring her back."

Sully pushed off the doorjamb and straightened as much as his old back would allow. His pale skin reddened as his face tightened. "You think it's that easy to make a huge golem that can withstand the forces of an entire universe? You think it was that simple last time for Elliot to use his abilities to even locate Darin? And for that matter, the only reason we could lure Darin to join with the golem — which didn't really happen the way we expected anyway — was because we had an item personal to him. Do we have an item personal to the little girl version of Maria? The only thing I can think of is Gram herself. Do you want to stick Gram inside of a golem and throw her into another universe?"

Roni cringed as she sat back on the edge of the bed. "I'm just trying to help think through this."

"You need to stop trying to help and start to learn by listening first. Once you've got the proper knowledge of what you're supposed to be doing, then you can help."

Elliot banged his cane on the floor. "We are not going to sit here and rehash these arguments over and over. It only helps our enemies. Now Sully, you must acknowledge that Roni is a novice and that perhaps you did make a mistake in sending her here. That was your fault. And you must own the repercussions of that choice." Sully started to argue but Elliot smacked his cane against Sully's shoulder. Before Roni could snicker, Elliot faced her. "You must accept that we know more than you. You do not like authority of any kind, and we understand that. You did not like it when Gram was in charge and you're now going to be upset with Sully because he is in charge. I have no doubt that if I were in charge, you would be angry with me as well. But at least admit that your anger, your real anger, is because you know you screwed up. You went against the orders and expectations that were given to you in some hope of being the hero and acting flashy or whatever was in your head. And because of that, we are in a dangerous situation."

Roni punched the side of the bed. "Maria is partly my mother. How was I supposed to let that go? Would you have ignored her if it was your mother?"

"If doing so meant hurting my living grandmother, the one who raised and cared for me, then perhaps I would. At the very least, I would have given her more consideration than you did. And I would've talked with my grandmother, asked her to help me understand why we shouldn't go help that sliver of my mother floating in another universe. Help me understand the kind of pain she may have endured seeing her daughter's double in that rift. Just plain understand. Own your mistakes, Roni. And you too, Sully."

Elliot's gaze drifted from one to the other before he walked out of the room shaking his head. Sully let Elliot pass, then leveled a hard glare at Roni. She braced herself for another tirade, but instead, he merely muttered as he turned away. There were a lot of good things to be said about Elliot's ability to heal, but Roni decided that this time around, she would have benefited from a little sympathy for her wounds, instead.

Alone in the room, she sat with her thoughts in the silence surrounding her. But then she heard that mewing again. Only this time it sounded louder — a tiny fraction but enough that she no longer thought the sound belonged to a cat. It was more than a simple meow. Rather, it had a longer flow to it like an ambulance siren far in the distance — but not a European ambulance. An American one — with its stretched-out tone rising and falling like a leaf floating on a wave.

Coupled to the sound, came the smell — a sickly-sweet aroma like cotton candy. Roni closed her eyes, attempting to dull all her senses but that of smell. She inhaled slowly, letting the aroma drift through her nose and down her throat. It was more than sugar. She smelled some type of soap.

Sugar. And soap. Like a little girl.

Roni's knee bounced, and she gripped the edge of the bed tight. She listened intently to the silence of the room. Feeling the rush of blood pumping through her head, she opened her mouth and with a cracking voice said, "Maria?"

She waited for a response but none came. Roni had never believed in ghosts, but then again, she had believed in there being only one universe. With the latter clearly wrong, perhaps the former could be true.

"Maria?" A little stronger this time.

Roni's shoulders convulsed back, slamming the shoulder

blades close to each other. Her head arched back. Like a mass of muscle spasms, it happened again. But nothing had struck her. Nobody had assaulted her. She had experienced a whack against her spine, but from the inside.

When that thought voiced in her head, her pulse shot up as if she had sprinted a hundred-meter dash. Sweat beaded across her skin. Her head throbbed and she felt nauseous.

She needed air. Stumbling to her feet, she made her way into the main part of the dorm. Elliot stood by the front door.

He glanced over at her and his face registered his concern. "You need to get back in bed."

"I need air."

Hobbling over on his cane, he said, "Then I will escort you."

"Leave me alone."

He tried to take her arm, but she wrenched it away. The sudden movement caused her to trip forward. Thankfully, she managed to stay upright. Refusing to look back — she did not want to see Elliot's pitying concern — she pushed on outside.

It was still dark. How was that possible? She glanced at her watch — 9:03 pm. She had been knocked out for a full day. More lost time. At least, she had the cool, fresh air to fill her lungs.

And it did feel good. But her heart still raced, her head still ached, and her skin still chilled. *Is this a panic attack?*

Squatting, she let her head hang and focused on breathing. After about a minute, she thought she might be feeling better. She rose, stretched her arms, and looked over to see the church.

Gram would be in there. No doubt about it. Roni considered following Elliot's advice and returning to bed. She did not want to talk with Sully, and she certainly did not want to face Gram.

But being a future leader of the Parallel Society meant facing the hard and difficult head on. She could think of nothing more difficult at the moment than dealing with Gram. And if she indeed had suffered a panic attack, then clearly Gram was at the heart of it. Better to get that taking care of before dealing with the trouble between universes.

Roni entered the church.

While the Abbey only served a handful of cultish nuns, it had been built with a larger audience in mind. Like many of the cathedrals in Ireland — Gothic architecture intended to praise the Lord through artistry and design — it's cavernous space overwhelmed and mystified the senses. As Roni shuffled down the center aisle of the nave, she had a moment of awe at the detailed beauty found in the grand architecture. Long columns led up to pointed arches, to windowed clearstory, to ribbed vaulting which kept the high ceiling from collapsing. At the apse of the Cathedral, an enormous stained-glass window depicting the Virgin Mary surrounded by rolling hills and beautiful animals created an intoxicating view. In front of it, a life-sized wooden carving of Jesus on the cross gazed down at the parishioners. Kneeling in the front pew, Gram had her fingers laced, her elbows leaning forward on the railing, and her head lowered in prayer.

Roni knelt next to her grandmother. She heard distant cries — more lost animals or something coming from inside? — but kept her head bowed out of respect for her grandmother's beliefs. At length, Gram put out her hand and held the top of Roni's.

"It's okay," Gram said.

Of all the things Gram could have uttered, all the ways she could have vented her anger, this pierced Roni's healed chest and drove straight through to her heart. Her head dropped to the wood railing, and she let her tears fall. "I'm so sorry. I only wanted to help you. Help her."

"That's why you are going to be very good at this job. One day."

Sniffling, Roni rubbed the tears from her eyes. "Sully doesn't think so."

"Of course he does. He's just angry at himself for making a poor decision and is angry because he wants to protect me. He thinks he's failed. That's part of the job being leader."

Roni gazed up at the statue of Jesus. Her top lip curled.

"Don't be like that," Gram said.

"What did I do?"

"Don't come in here and look upon the Church with such disdain."

"I wasn't. Honest. I was thinking that it must've been hard for him. He's like Maria — stuck between worlds. Right? He was a mortal man but also a heavenly being."

"I suppose."

"I wonder — you think when people talk about feeling his presence, that they really physically feel something?"

"Of course."

"Well, we still have the book that Maria was pulled into. Maybe we can find a way to feel her presence. To bring her back."

Roni's skin tightened. *Another panic attack?*

"Dear, it's a sweet thought, but no. I have finally, truly lost my daughter."

Roni's body shuddered. Straight to the bone. The muscles on the back of her neck contracted. As if Maria had screamed the word *No!* and it threatened to rip Roni to pieces.

With a production of grunts and groans, Gram rose to her feet and settled back on the pew bench. "Sit with me."

Roni did not move at first. She feared her legs would not support her. She needed time alone to consider what had happened to her — continued to happen — but the expectant look on Gram's face meant any other plans had to be postponed. With grunts and groans of her own, she managed to get to the bench.

Gram folded her hands across her large bosom and offered Roni a genuine smile. "I know you meant well. I really do. But I want you to listen closely. I'm going to tell you a story about your mother, back when she was only nine years old, back before she ever came to this place."

The mixed odor of sugar and soap returned to fill the air. Roni had to take shallow breaths in order not to choke.

Gram said, "Your mother was a sweet, wonderful little girl. But she always had that wild side, too. The two forces battled within her all of the time. If we went to an amusement park, part of her would want to go on the roller coasters — even though she did not meet the height requirement. She didn't care. The other part of her did. The other part of her stopped her from begging to go. And yet, I would catch her eyeing those roller coasters. I could see part of her brain trying to figure out how she could get away with sneaking on for a ride yet also make sure that I would never know. And more importantly, nobody would.

"Of course, with roller coasters at amusement parks, she never stood a chance. Nobody would let her ride, and she would have to go home feeling a little left out. Yet she also seemed a bit relieved — that by following the rules, she had somehow done better.

"But there were other times when opportunities presented themselves to her. Those times her wild side won out."

Roni's head swirled, and she strained to keep focus on Gram's story. She attempted to hold her face stoic so as not to betray any discomfort, anything out of the ordinary. She probably failed, but she also figured Gram was too wrapped up in our own tale to notice.

"Once," Gram said, her voice darkening as her eyes gazed off toward the transept, "Maria and I went for a short hike and a picnic lunch at the park. It was a beautiful day — crisp air, golden leaves everywhere, perfect. Near the end of the hike, we came upon a dead squirrel. It caught Maria's attention because its belly had bloated up. She thought it looked like one of those toys that when you squeezed it, the eyes bulged out. I told her not to touch it and then moved along. Later, we sat on a blanket and had a lovely picnic. There were other families around, other children, and this was at a time when parents were not scared to let their children explore. So, while Maria and some of the other kids ran off to the woods or to play ball on the fields, I sat back with the other adults and chatted."

Gram smirked as the memory played out in her head.

"She would've gotten away with it, but she scared some of the other kids. They ratted her out. I learned that Maria went back to the squirrel. She found a stick and using a rock, she sharpened it. Nothing deadly, just enough to poke that squirrel's belly. Some of the other children who had been equally fascinated warned her not to do it. Their parents had also told them not to touch the dead animal. But she didn't listen.

"That's all. I never found out what else happened because all the screaming kids got their parents worked up, and I had to usher Maria away. I didn't want to make her feel bad for being inquisitive, so I let the matter go. But I want you to understand — she was not a perfect person. Not even from the beginning. And when that rift did what it did to her, it exacerbated the problem. That's the thing that you saw as Maria, the thing I wanted to think of as my daughter —it never was. It looked like her, but she never was whatever idealized version of her you have in your head. Never was what was in my head." Gram leaned forward, took Roni's hand, and kissed it. "She never could be. You understand?"

A harrowing shriek attacked Roni's ears. Bile flooded her throat, burning as it raced up and back down, and left behind an acrid, sick taste. Her head pounded with images from a little girl's twisted picnic afternoon.

Roni saw that squirrel — a bloated carcass, soulless and stiff. She could feel the girl's determination — using a dull rock to sharpen the stick. Fascination motivated some of her actions, but cruelty and defiance were at the core. A twisted sense of satisfaction flooded her as the gases poured out of the hole in the squirrel's belly making a wet, high tone like the mouth of a balloon held mostly closed.

"I'm sorry," Roni managed to say without throwing up. "I need to be by myself."

She hurried to her feet and rushed down the long nave until she reached the exit. She could feel Gram staring at her in confusion. Those eyes pressed upon her back hot and uncomfortable.

Once outside, she looked for privacy. She thought about returning to the lake but figured Gram might come searching for her there. The dorms and library were out — she had no desire to see either building ever again. She recalled seeing a barn further up the road from the dorms; however, she did not know if that building belonged to the Abbey or if they bordered a farm. She did not want to add trespassing to her list of transgressions this trip.

Instead, she opted to take the path leading from the library into the woods. Worst case, it was a nature trail that made a big circle. She would end up right back here, but at least, she would have time to think in the quiet. However, after a few minutes of walking, she discovered it led to the Abbey cemetery. While that held a touch of gruesome irony, it also guaranteed some solitude. She'd take it.

Walking along the path, she tried to clear her thoughts. It was a foolish attempt. No way could she stop thinking about what she had experienced since waking up.

The sounds that plagued her. The headaches and body aches. But mostly, the sense of being communicated to by word, by feeling, and by image.

Something must have happened when those energy pulses from the rift hit her. Somehow, she had connected with Maria.

Perhaps Maria's presence within the universe of the book had somehow leeched into this new connection with Roni. Or perhaps Maria never left at all. Perhaps what remained of her had been scattered into the very air Roni breathed.

Rubbing her temples, she moaned. The path opened onto the graveyard — a small but functional plot of land devoted to rows upon rows of nuns who had served the Abbey well. These people sure loved to bury themselves in a variety of ways.

Roni walked to the opposite side where she found a large oak tree. Sitting down at the base, leaning her back against its trunk, she continued her attempts to make sense out of what had happened. She needed more than simple suppositions. She needed to know the truth.

Time drifted by — she lost track. Her thoughts swam in a murky darkness that would have shrouded her even at high noon. Perhaps, she thought, she had fallen asleep for a short time, but the pain in her head had not eased — usually a rest made headaches disappear for her.

Roni got back to her feet. Might as well return. Time to find out what the Old Gang wanted to do.

But before Roni set out, she saw several lights coming her way. She heard the steady beat of an old drum. Out of the deep shadows of the woods, Sister Mary led a procession of the Abbey nuns. Three of them carried a coffin while Sister Mary hit the wide, shallow drum with a bone. As they entered the graveyard, flashlights bounced from ropes around their necks and their habits rustled the ground. The drum beat out a mournful sound.

But the procession did not stop. They went beyond the cemetery, deeper into the woods. Not following a well-trodden path but forging into an unmarked section.

Roni did not know what to make of what she saw but one thought echoed in her head as she quietly followed them — *this isn't right.*

CHAPTER 12

Leading the way, Sister Mary had no trouble creating a path through the woods despite the dark. The nuns followed her without question, though the casket made travel awkward, forcing them to weave around the denser groupings of trees. Still, they managed to stay close to Sister Mary more often than not. Behind it all, Roni darted from tree to tree. Not that the nuns would spot her in the dark, but she still thought precautions were the smart play. When the woods opened into a clearing, Roni stayed behind a tree trunk to watch from a distance.

Large stones cut like massive blocks prescribed a circle within the clearing. Some of the stones acted like oversized benches while others stood upright to form the impression of walls. On the sides of the vertical stones, Roni spotted markings — possibly Gaelic writings. Finally, after Sister Claudia started a fire in the pit dug near the middle of the circle, Roni understood — this was a pagan burial. From the soft flicker of orange firelight, her thoughts were confirmed when she noticed the graves lining the back half of the clearing.

Off to her left, two trees kissed up against each other

forming a wider barrier. Roni scurried across, her heart hammering, certain every crinkling, leaf-breaking step would be her undoing. But she reached the trees. Even before peeking around the trunk, this new position allowed her to hear clearly what Sister Mary said.

"My dear sisters," Sister Mary began, "we have much to do tonight. But as we prepare to step forward into a new chapter of the Abbey, we must first turn the page on the old chapter."

The three sisters set the coffin on the ground and bowed their heads. "Sister Ashley was a dear woman to us all. It may seem that she was taken too early from us, but the Lord has a plan for all, and it is our duty to have faith rather than sadness. We few of the Abbey are the chosen. That comes with great responsibilities and greater dangers. Sister Ashley's sacrifice is of both."

Roni rolled back behind the two trunks. Glancing upward, she noticed several points where the trees left a gap. She pulled out her phone, set the camera to film, made sure to cut off the camera light, and lined up a good shot between the trees.

"Tonight, we honor Sister Ashley in the best way we can." Sister Mary stepped closer to the coffin. With a twitch of her finger, Sister Claudia and Sister Susan opened the lid. "Without a body, we must mourn her through representation." Sister Mary pulled out an old Bible — leather bound and valuable from the looks of it. She set it in the coffin with care. "She always admired this copy I kept on my desk. It is my great honor to bury it as a sign of my love and devotion to one of our fallen."

Sister Susan stepped forward. She pulled out a thin, gold necklace with a crucifix pendant. "She did not think we noticed, but she prayed more and harder than any I have ever seen. She even gave Sister Rachel a run." The nuns tittered. "I give her this so that she may continue to do so up in Heaven."

Sister Rachel went next, placing a rosary in the coffin. "I had only begun to know her, but no nun should be without this."

Finally, with a nod from Sister Mary, Sister Claudia approached the coffin. "Sister Ashley was dear to me. Just as I am a pupil under Sister Mary, I hoped one day for Sister Ashley to be my pupil. Her love of knowledge and enthusiasm for her faith left me in awe at times. I'm afraid I have nothing to place in there because the things she meant most to me cannot be represented physically. Her passion, her love, her caring."

"You are wrong," Sister Mary said. "You do have something to give."

She reached into her pocket and pulled out a tissue. After a few dabs at Sister Claudia's wet cheeks, she handed over the tear-stained tissue. Sister Claudia smiled as more tears fell. She placed the tissue in the coffin.

Another twitch of Sister Mary's finger and the lid returned. Sister Mary said, "Please Sister Susan, make sure that our groundskeepers see to the burying."

"Ay, ma'am."

"Good. Then it is time. Come forth."

Sister Claudia and Sister Susan stepped forward and kneeled. Sister Susan jerked her head to beckon Sister Rachel over. Once all three nuns knelt before Sister Mary, they bowed their heads.

"Tonight, as we mourn the loss of one, we celebrate the creation of another." Sister Mary stepped over and placed her hands atop Sister Rachel's head. "Becoming a permanent member of this Abbey is no small matter and not to be taken lightly. Heaven speaks to us. While it is true that we call the energy beneath the church a conduit, it is more of a mechanism. Because *we* are the conduit. The Angels speak through us, and in doing so, we take on the responsibility of spreading their message throughout the world. Even when that message must be kept secret. It can be a confusing conflict within, a great balancing act which will test the limits of your conscience and control, one that requires great amounts of prayer, one that will stretch your calling far greater than any other experience any other church could provide, and one I know you are fully capable of handling."

"Ay, Sister. I am ready."

Sister Mary sidestepped to the right and rested her hands upon Sister Susan's head. "To join me requires the greatest devotion for it is permanent. Like the ring you wear to symbolize your devotion to Jesus, this appointment can never be torn asunder. If you accept my blessing tonight, you will be with this Abbey until the day you die. And possibly even after that. You must be willing to walk the narrow path of your faith with the conviction of one who knows the truth. Because you have seen it. It may seem an easy choice — what nun would turn away the chance to speak with angels? But the sacrifices required will bring upon your shoulders the greatest weights you've ever felt. The loyalty required is enormous. You will never look at the world the same because you will see all those people out there who think they know better than you, and you won't be able to tell them a thing."

"I'm ready, Sister." Sister Susan said.

Roni readjusted her position against the tree, but she did not feel uncomfortable from holding the camera up. No. She heard too much in Sister Mary's speech that sounded familiar.

Sister Mary sidestepped again, placing her hands upon Sister Claudia's head. "Leadership is a difficult and lonely path. It requires devotion and loyalty, yet also a sense of duty greater than that of self-preservation. I have done all I can to prepare you. I had intended to teach you more before today, but I never expected you and Sister Ashley to hasten this moment."

As Sister Mary continued speaking words that Roni had heard coming from Gram's mouth in one version or another, something brushed the tree limbs in the woods. Roni paused her camera and brought it down to her eye. Using the zoom function, she scanned the woods.

She expected to see Sully vigorously waving her away from this scene. When she did not spot a human shape, she thought she might come across a deer or elk or some other large animal that had accidently stumbled upon the service. But again, she saw nothing.

When she finally located the source of the noise, her lips parted but no sound came from her closed throat. Three purple-black balls of smoke hovered just beyond the tree line. They were from the rift. Roni recalled seeing them dart out — one of the last things she remembered before being knocked unconscious. They did not belong in this universe, and that made them relics. They also appeared to be alive which meant they were living relics.

The way those creatures from the rift waited (the word *rifters* popped into Roni's mind), the way they appeared to be watching the nuns — it left Roni with a sense of threat. She couldn't let the nuns stay there and become targets, but she had no idea what these rifters could do. One thing she had learned from her previous encounters with creatures from other universes — knowledge of the enemy meant everything. If they even were enemies.

She moved toward the edge of the tree trunks with the intent of warning the nuns. They would not be happy to see her, they would probably yell at her for invading their privacy, they might even take their anger out on the Society. But at least they would not suffer at the whims of these living relics. Yet as she moved, sharp pain dug into her spine.

Placing a hand on her lower back, she inhaled sharply — the smell of sugar and soap filled her nostrils. She rolled back against the trunk, pressing her spine against the hard wood.

Maria? she thought. Warmth flushed over her skin like sinking into a hot bath. Tears welled in Roni's eyes, and she clutched her mouth for fear of crying out loud.

As her mind raced through the possibilities, Sister Claudia's raised voice cut into the air. "To the angels waiting on the edge of our circle, please come forth. We welcome you. We love you and are ready to receive you."

CHAPTER 13

The shock stunned Roni straight through to the ends of her limbs. She stood by the kissing trees with her head in full view should anyone look over. But even if her mind had thought to take cover, she could not. The sight before her brooked no argument towards looking away.

At Sister Claudia's call, the three purple-black creatures, the rifters, floated into the circle. The dark smoke around each one dripped off like melting wax. When the smoke hit the forest floor, it puffed and dissipated — only acting like actual smoke at that final moment. The rifters spread out, one behind each kneeling nun, and simply hovered. No sounds. No sense of sentience. Nothing to suggest thought or intention. Yet Roni's stomach turned for those ladies.

Sister Claudia stood and joined Sister Mary. "Look behind you. These are angels."

Sister Susan whipped her head around while Sister Rachel took a more hesitant approach. Both yelped.

"Do not be afraid," Sister Claudia went on. "These are angels in their true form. Not the fanciful and majestic images painted by human artists over the centuries, but their real, angelic appearance. Revel in their mysterious beauty and know that it is our divine purpose to host these immaculate beings. We will give them human form so that they may perform Heaven's duties here on Earth."

Dashing tears from her eyes, Sister Claudia returned to kneel with the others. She bowed her head. "Sister Mary, I beg your forgiveness. There were some moments — after Sister Ashley and I had reopened the conduit — moments where I lost my way. Worse still, after Sister Ashley succumbed to the conduit, I faltered. My faith abandoned me. But only for a moment. I gave voice to my fear and doubt, yet when I saw you on the stairs, I remembered why I had come all this way in my life. It will never happen again. Please, please, forgive me."

Sister Mary cocked her head to the side and smiled with such benevolence that those kneeling before her leaned back as if under the heavy rays of the sun. But Roni could see that smile, too — a hideous, macabre mask.

"We all seek the day that Heaven can spread across the Earth," Sister Mary said. "And it is only understandable and human that you would want to hasten the day. But as Sister Ashley demonstrated, the mighty purity of Heaven will destroy us all if allowed to break free. I have known this for decades. So, we must wait." Spreading her arms to include all the nuns, she went on, "This has always been our divine duty. For centuries, the nuns of the Abbey have kept the conduit stable to ensure our communication with the Angels and to make certain that the great strength of Heaven does not destroy all which we cherish but rather makes it beautiful. We all knew that someday this moment would arrive, when the Angels could leave the conduit and join us. It happened once before — centuries ago, and it led to the schism between Sisters Margaret and Agnes. It happened a second time — more recently, in fact. When it happened to me."

With gasps that came close to equaling their surprise at seeing the Angels, the nuns murmured to each other as they kept their eyes upon Sister Mary.

"I was quite young. I had only been a nun for a few years. I joined the Abbey, and after only a week, I was brought downstairs to see the conduit, to learn my duties in helping maintain it. Like many of you, I spent my early years with night duty, and it was on the fourth night that an angel came to me. Just like those floating behind you now, this angel slipped out of the conduit and floated before me. Turned out that one of the books the Parallel Society had provided did not do its job properly. And for that, I am so grateful.

"I offered myself to this angel, instinctually understanding that it needed my body as its host, but then it slipped back into the conduit — apparently the faulty book worked a little bit, after all.

"But when the Parallel Society sent Lillian Donaugh and her daughter, everything changed. The angel pulled part of little Maria into the conduit and in doing so, it created an exchange. The angel left Maria behind and it was able to join our world permanently. It came to me right away and has been with me ever since."

The kneeling nuns gazed up at Sister Mary with pale-faced awe.

"That's right. I am an angel. And in all the years since I joined with Sister Mary, I have tried to find a safe way to release more of my angelic compatriots. It is why I encouraged Sister Ashley to research our past with the Abbey. I knew she was smart, and she would be able to find the mythic book Sister Agnes stole. Oh, indeed, I knew she would sneak down into the tombs and spend time in the study. I relished the moment when she would figure out how to find and utilize the book down there. Sister Claudia, you've asked for forgiveness, but you will not get it. You have no need for it. You have done such marvelous work. You deserve praise."

"Thank you," Sister Claudia stuttered.

"The time has arrived. Pray and accept this gift from the Lord. Allow these angels entry, become one with them, so that we may take the next steps into bringing about a more heavenly world."

Sister Rachel leaned her head back and spread her lips wide. "I am ready."

"Wonderful. Give yourself to the angel, willingly allow the union. Once we are all angels, we shall return to the conduit what was taken so that it can be stabilized once again."

"I thought the books stabilized the conduit," Sister Claudia said.

"It was the child's essence, not the foolish Parallel Society books. Before Maria gave herself to the conduit, the books were all we had — unreliable at best."

Sister Susan cleared her throat. "Excuse me, but did not Sister Claudia prove the wait is over? There are three angels here — more than ever before. More than have ever even been seen. Perhaps the time to release the conduit completely has come."

"Possibly," Sister Mary said. "If so, all the more reason to stabilize the conduit. We want it to hold together as long as possible so that we can pull in the greatest number of angels. Yes. Good thinking. We must prepare."

Sister Susan lifted her head back, closed her eyes, and awaited the arrival of her angel. Sister Claudia did the same, and Roni could see the scowl on her face. That nun did not like being shown up — especially by another nun.

Without any signal or word, the three smoky masses floated over the faces of the nuns. As they lowered, appearing to be inhaled, each one of the Sisters gave out a pleasurable moan. Out of context, Roni supposed the joining of Angel and human made a rather sexual sound — even pornographic. But watching it happen filled her with dread.

A four-note sequence chimed from Roni's phone. The darn thing wanted to be helpful by notifying her that one of her friends had posted a cat picture or perhaps one of the games she played needed an update. The four nuns — now part-Angel — turned in unison to face the tree Roni stood near. They saw her face. They knew she had been watching.

Roni whirled around and darted off into the woods.

CHAPTER 14

Roni bolted through the pathless woods, snaking her way around one tree, then another, careening in the direction she hoped would lead her back to the Abbey proper. Even after she realized that the nuns could not run fast enough with their long tunics dragging in the dark of the woods, she continued to push on as quickly as possible. When she broke from the tree line, she dashed across the grass, passing the church, and headed straight for the dormitory.

Elliot stood by the doorway like a serene statue gazing at the night sky. "What's the matter?"

"Inside," she said as she rushed by him and entered the dorm.

Sully started at her sudden appearance. He snapped a book shut and hid it behind his back. Once his face registered recognition of Roni, he relaxed. "Do you want me to have a heart attack?"

Roni paused as she gazed at the poorly hidden book. She then glanced back at the doorway. "You had Elliot standing watch for you. What are you up to?"

"Just trying to get a better understanding of the women who live here." From behind his back, Sully produced

Sister Ashley's diary.

Elliot walked in. "What happened? The look on your face —"

"After you both secured the rift, after you healed me, did you use your cane to scan my body?"

"My cane does not —"

"You know what I mean. However you do it, did you do it?"

"There hasn't been time and I did not observe any symptoms that would suggest the need. Why?"

Roni rushed over to the nearest window and peeked outside. "They'll be here soon. Listen carefully, and don't ask questions. Just believe me."

Her urgency had the desired effect. Sully and Elliot huddled in close, sitting on the edges of two beds, and they listened. Roni described everything she had witnessed in the woods and showed the video on her phone as well. With her heart racing, she continued to take periodic glances out the window.

"Look, I know I screwed up and that I made you angry." Roni turned toward Sully. "You can yell at me later. Right now, what are we supposed to do?"

His face paled, and his nose wrinkled as if Roni had spoken a foreign language. He walked the length of the dorm with his fingers dancing against each other under his chin. On his return trip, Roni could see the way his deep concentration mixed with his pale fear.

The urge to rush over to this old man, grab him by the shoulders, and shake him into making a decision flooded Roni's overflowing thoughts. The nuns moved slowly but they weren't sloths. Soon enough, they would arrive. Why didn't he give any orders?

"It's okay," Elliot said, moving to the side of his good friend. "I'm sure Lillian had the same troubles her first time."

His first time? She had not considered it before, but Elliot spotted the problem right away. Sully had become their leader during a moment of crisis. Decisions had already been made and he reacted to them. But after that, for close to a year, they had lived without any real trouble. All had been quiet. This was the first time they faced a situation where he had to make all the decisions.

As understanding came to her, Roni missed Elliot's quiet words to Sully. But she saw Sully nod his head and offer a weak smile.

Patting Elliot on the shoulder, Sully said, "I think it would be best if you go find Gram and bring her here. We need the team together."

"That sounds like a good idea." With orders given, Elliot rushed out of the room.

Sully readjusted his glasses and settled on the edge of the bed.

"That's it?" Roni said, gazing out the window once again.

"Your Gram is the only one of us who has had regular contact with these nuns. She's our best source of information on how to deal with them."

"When Elliot gets back with Gram, it'll be too late. We won't have time to hear what her thoughts are because those nuns will be on us. I don't see them right now, but I'm telling you they were not that far behind me."

Stamping his foot, Sully said, "I know, I know." Holding his mouth tight, he removed his glasses and rubbed his eyes. "I apologize. I didn't mean to snap at you. With all that we had to do to keep the rift from exploding, well, I'm a bit exhausted."

Roni sat next to Sully and wrapped her arms around him. "It's okay. We're all on edge. I might even be a bit scared. If we were back home, if I could be under the bookstore in that beautiful library, then I'd find out what we needed to know about these creatures and that would make me feel better prepared."

"Instead, you have to rely on me and worst of all, your grandmother."

"I can rely on you all just fine. You've all saved the universe enough times to earn that." Roni surveyed the room as she spoke. "So, the current plan is that Elliot is going to find Gram and bring her back. And we're hoping she will know something about what's going on with the nuns. That's what we're doing, right?"

Sully shrugged. "It's all we've got for the moment."

"Then we're going to need more time."

He raised his head. "You look like you have an idea."

"A stupid one, but it's better than nothing." Roni took one last peek outside — still no nuns were visible, but she could hear their voices. The words were garbled at this distance, but she could not mistake the gleeful threat of Sister Claudia.

Roni and Sully worked together to move the beds into the center of the room. They formed a circle and cleared out the middle. She stepped back to look at their work. Not terribly convincing, but they were out of time. She heard footsteps heading up to the door.

Sister Claudia and Sister Rachel stepped into the dorm with hands on hips like twin conquerors. Roni expected as much from Sister Claudia, but Sister Rachel was a different matter. From first arriving at the Abbey, Roni had seen little of Sister Rachel yet still built an impression of a meek people-pleaser who posed no threat. However, seeing the woman stand shoulder-to-shoulder with Sister Claudia, framed by the stark white wimple and shadowed by the dark black habit, Sister Rachel promised to be an imposing force.

Sister Claudia clasped her hands behind her back as she stepped forward. But where Sully had looked frightened and thoughtful, Sister Claudia looked downright terrifying. "You did a sinful thing."

"Hope you're not looking for an apology," Roni said, willing to say anything to keep the conversation going. They simply had to stall long enough for Elliot and Gram to arrive. At least, she told herself as much. The other voice inside her head promised that no amount of stalling would help.

"Words from a devil are never to be trusted — especially if they are words you no longer need to hear. Besides, you don't strike me as the kind what wants to make amends. No, with you, I only see an obstruction. Saw it when you first drove up here. Even told Sister Mary we should be done with you. You ask me, I say the days of working with the Parallel Society should have ended a long time ago."

"I might actually care if you were really Sister Claudia. Probably not, but I might."

"You see?" Sister Claudia gazed back at Sister Rachel. "Do you? They have no concept of Angels. No idea how to deal with us." Gesturing to the circle of beds, she added, "This is cute. Did you intend this to frighten us or are you offering us a nice place to rest?"

Sully tugged on Roni's arm, pulling her closer to the center of the circle. In a voice full of confidence, he said, "This is a circle of Darsha. If you are what you say you are, then crossing into the circle will cause excruciating pain to both your body and your eternal soul."

Roni's face locked in grim defiance. Anything less and she might have smirked at the ridiculousness of Sully's bluff. The best part — the bluff was also brilliant. If these women truly believed themselves to have communed with Angels, then they would not cross into the circle for fear of hurting their souls. But should they take that dangerous step into the circle, then their faith might be shaken when nothing happened — proving they were not angels.

The dilemma would hold them for a short time. Eventually, they would figure out that a circle of beds was nothing more than a circle of beds. That the circle of Darsha did not exist.

Sister Claudia meandered along the edge of the circle. She snarled at Roni. "I truly despise you."

"Feeling is mutual."

"That right there. That's one of the reasons. You come in here with this arrogant attitude as if you know anything that's been going on round these parts. I watched how you spoke with your grandmother. Set aside the respect you should show first simply because she is an elder and your own blood, but you should respect her opinion because she has been dealing with the conduit longer than you or I have been alive. You should show respect to Sister Mary because she has been dealing with it longer than any of us — even your Gram. And you should show me some respect because I've lived with this thing every day for years. And what are you? Nothing more than an apprentice who hasn't even spent forty-eight hours here. Yet you think you know everything, that you're qualified to understand anything you see. Pathetic, really."

She reached the far side of the circle and nudged the edge with her foot. Sister Rachel mirrored the actions on the other side.

"I have prayed a lot since your arrival," Sister Claudia continued. "I've been trying to understand why the Lord brought you into my life. What good could possibly come from such arrogant ignorance as yours? For a while, I thought Sister Ashley had it right — that you were here for us to use, so that we could use that powerful book without breaking our vows — that we might open the rift.

"But I was wrong.

"You see, I have respect for Sister Mary. She has shown me the error of my thinking. Our job is not to force open the rift but to help it grow and become stronger so that it can come forth when it is ready."

The more Sister Claudia spoke, the more Roni thought the magic circle bluff had been a mistake. Suddenly it no longer felt like a shield. Rather, it had become a prison. Hoping she still had some bravery in her voice, she said, "Why are you calling it a rift? I thought it was a conduit to Heaven."

With a bemused toss of her head, Sister Claudia said, "Did I? Things really are changing rapidly. Which makes me think that the idea mulling around in my head might not be so crazy after all. The Lord brought you to us, and the Lord sent us the Angels as well. I will trust these thoughts for they are guided by his angels and his will."

Though Roni really did not want to hear the answer, she still asked, "What is it the Lord's telling you?"

"Sister Mary always said that after the child had been partially taken into the rift, all became better, more stable than ever before. If you had any respect for your elders, your Gram would tell you that I'm speaking the truth. Since you are also a blood relation, then perhaps your blood will help the rift regain its strength."

"You want my blood?"

"Maybe. Maybe it's your heart. Or your bones or your brain. I don't know. We'll just have to throw you into the rift and pray for the best."

Though Sully could not stand straight, he still knew how to intimidate with his voice. "Enough. We have been polite and respectful by allowing you to have your say. Now, you will listen to us."

At least, Roni always thought Sully sounded intimidating. But she had been a little girl growing up in the family bookstore — all of the Old Gang had intimidated her. Sister Claudia, however, had no such history with Sully.

She reached down and threw aside one of the beds. "I take no commands from you."

From behind, Roni heard Sister Rachel doing the same. Sully stepped in front of Roni. He pushed backwards and to the side so that neither Sister Claudia nor Sister Rachel was behind them. "Stay where you are. I'm warning you."

Roni had no doubt the Sisters heard the shake in Sully's voice. Roni had heard it. She also had no doubt Sully shared the same thought that plagued her mind — *Where the hell were Gram and Elliot?*

Sister Rachel snorted a laugh. "The little old man is afraid of us."

"I am not afraid of a couple nuns."

"Oh, old man, we are so much more than nuns."

The Sisters stepped forward. Their eyes glowed deep emerald. As if in a choreographed dance, both raised their arms, and together, they lifted off the ground. Not far — only about a foot — but hovering nuns were still hovering nuns. Roni's heart dropped to her stomach. Any chance that Sully's bluff would continue to stop them vanished.

Sister Rachel swooped in and clawed at Sully. Thick, green veins pulsed on her face. She slammed down, clearly expecting to toss him aside, only to find that she would have had an easier time moving a steel bridge. As she swept across, her left arm lagged behind, pushing on his shoulder the extra seconds her brain needed to register the solid object she had hit.

Roni saw the woman's shoulder dislocate as she went

lurching into the beds. She whimpered in confusion as she rubbed her shoulder.

Sully spread his arms back, and Roni inched closer. She pressed her chest against his back. His voice had been shaking but his body remained a mountain against all storms.

The nuns' next attack proved to Roni that the creatures inside them were somehow linked together. No way could the women have coordinated their next move without such a thing.

Sister Claudia floated higher as if she might flow overhead and land behind. This forced Sully to lift his legs in order to reposition, and the moment his firm connection to the ground ended, Sister Rachel appeared from below. She barreled into Sully, screaming as the pain ignited in her shoulder, and knocked them aside. Sister Claudia flew in and grabbed hold of Roni.

"I'm going to enjoy watching you fall into the rift," Sister Claudia said. "In fact, I'm going to ..."

She stared at Roni — stared *into* Roni. Those frosty, emerald eyes set Roni's skin tingling. Roni wanted to look away but remained locked on the nun's gaze. She felt Sister Claudia's fingers pressing into her skin, and it took a great act of will to avoid vomiting. Or crying, for that matter.

But then the nun's eyes widened. "Halt!" Sister Claudia pointed at Sister Rachel to make sure the command had been obeyed. For her part, Sister Rachel had Sully's arms pinned behind the poor man.

"What? I'm having fun."

"I see into you," Sister Claudia said to Roni. "I know what's inside you. Hiding away in there."

Roni felt Maria cringing, searching for an escape even though there was none.

With a disappointed frown, Sister Claudia said, "I guess

I won't get to throw you into the rift. Not just yet, anyway."

"Why not?" Sister Rachel said. "What's happening over there?"

"You don't to get to ask me questions. Something has changed and it might help our cause. That's all you need to know. I'll discuss it with Sister Mary."

Roni couldn't help herself. "Still trying to one up Sister Susan?"

Before she even knew what had happened, Roni's face stung from the nun's sharp backhand.

"Sister Rachel, I want you to take both of these foolish heathens to the tombs. Lock them away with the dead until I have a chance to confer with Sister Mary."

Sister Rachel's green-veined grin promised to haunt Roni with nightmares for a long time to come.

CHAPTER 15

The door leading from the Abbey library to the tombs beneath closed with a thick thud. Roni slumped on the bottom stair and rested her head against the cool stone wall. Sully stood a few feet away taking in his surroundings.

As he kicked at the dusty floor, he rubbed his backside. "I do not care for these nuns at all."

"Jokes?" Roni uttered the word with more bite than she had intended. But if she held back, she thought tears would flow — for now, she'd rather be angry. "I've screwed everything up, remember? A little bit ago, you were fuming mad at me. Now, you're making jokes?"

"A little bit ago, the worst things I had to deal with were your screw ups and your attitude." Sully paused his inspection to lay a comforting hand on her head. "If you recall, a few minutes ago, I was stumbling through my first big moment as leader like a bar mitzvah boy delivering his sermon in front of his family."

"But now?"

"Ah, now is quite different. I have been trapped before. I've been held hostage, too. I've faced monsters — though never monstrous nuns but what's the big difference, really?

The details might be new, but being stuck in a troubling and dangerous situation — that's fairly standard for the Parallel Society. Goes with the job."

Roni chuckled. Then sniffled. Then wiped aside a tear. She thrust to her feet and stomped back up the stairs. Banging on the door, she said, "Open up! Let us out!"

"Stop with all that racket," Sully said from below. "You really think they'll let us go after all they did to put us here?"

"I'm not going to sit around waiting for Sister Mary to decide it's a good idea to throw us into the rift."

"No, that wouldn't be good, either. Lucky for you, you've got me. Now, come sit down here again and let me think. We need to prepare."

With reluctant steps, Roni returned. "You have a plan?"

"I will soon, if you stop distracting me."

As she sat, Roni watched Sully think. He lasted less than ten seconds.

"You can't stare at me. How am I supposed to come up with a plan if you're staring at me?"

"Sorry," she said. "It's not all on you, though. I can come up with a plan, too."

"I don't think that's what we need from you."

Rather than argue, Roni lowered her head. She could feel Sully staring at her, now, and she did not like it. The longer he said nothing, the heavier his stare pressed against her. At first, she thought he merely wanted her to understand the difficulty of solving their dilemma while another teammate waits expectantly. But after a moment, she peeked up.

His brow rose even as his mouth turned down. He had let the planning slip aside. Something else rested in that look.

No, Roni thought, *I can't lie to myself. I know exactly what he's waiting for.*

Still, she refused to lift her head, refused to let the thought congeal into words. The cool darkness of the tomb wrapped around her like gentle snowfall. Cold comfort, but better than facing the myriad of problems surrounding them.

"Roni." His gentle nudge slammed into her.

"Okay, okay. What do you really need to know? You heard Sister Claudia. You're a smart man. Can't you figure it all out? Do I have to say it?"

As he often did, Sully read the moment right. He started rummaging along the walls yet continued to talk with her. "If we're going to make it through this day, then yes — you need to tell me all the specifics. It's usually the details that make the difference." He glanced up the stairs. "From the quiet, I'm guessing we'll be stuck here for a bit. You might as well get the whole thing off your chest."

Roni laughed. A deep, hearty laugh. This hunched, little man could remain so calm at the precise time she needed it. Maybe he had more special powers than she realized. She gulped and her chest tightened. She felt like a teenager about to admit that she had taken drugs or had gotten knocked up or some other possibly life-altering event.

"Maria never fell into that book. I held onto her as long as I could and when I thought I let go of her, the rift happened, and well, I don't know exactly how it went down, but she's inside me."

"Oh."

Sully's boredom tripped up Roni's thoughts. Still, she went on, "Yes, well, I can hear her in my head. Not much. Not like sentences. But sounds and feelings. I can feel her on my skin. She reacts to the things she knows about."

"I see."

He stuck his head and arms into the nearest alcove. He

pulled out the bones of a long-deceased nun and placed them in a pile against the wall as he continued his macabre work.

"Why are you not taking this seriously?" Roni said, making no effort to hide her anger.

Using the flashlight on his phone, Sully squatted down to access the lower alcove. As he continued removing bones, he said, "I am taking this seriously. And I appreciate you not telling Gram about this."

"I wouldn't dare. I can see how hard it has been for her with everything that's happened. There is no reason to hurt her more. But I thought you should know. As leader. I thought you would find it important."

Poking his head out of the alcove, he dropped a thick femur onto the ground. "I understand that you think you have part of Maria in you. I also understand that you think it's important. And it might be. There's nothing I can do about it at the moment because, in case you missed it, we are trapped down here."

"There's no need to be nasty. I'm telling you this because when Sister Claudia grabbed me, she reacted to what she saw — namely, Maria. That's why she didn't throw us into the rift right away. She thinks — I don't know what she thinks, but it can't be good."

Scanning the area with his phone, Sully went on, "You've been with the Society long enough now to understand that there are all kinds of creatures out there. I fully believe that you have felt the things you say, and that you've experienced them in the way you say they happened. That does not mean that is what happened. Only a short while ago, you showed me a video of purple floating creatures —"

"That's right. And they went inside the nuns."

Sully paused and looked straight at Roni. "That is what

you saw, but it may not be what happened."

"But I saw it."

"Instead of being ingested, or somehow melding into the nuns for that matter, these creatures may only look that way. In fact, they may exist on multiple planes. We've encountered similar things before. They look like they're gone, but in reality, they hover around you, wear themselves upon you like bizarre clothing. They might be mimicking your feelings towards Maria instead of being Maria. You understand?" He brushed his hands on his pants. "All I'm asking that you do is consider the possibility that what you think to be the case might be wrong. Do that. And please, don't mention this again — especially if Gram can hear. Okay?"

Roni nodded. She did not agree with Sully — in fact, she knew she was right. She could feel it deep in her bones — but she would honor Sully's request nonetheless. At least, for now.

In a simple, yet blatant attempt to change the subject, she said, "What are you looking for?"

Sully snapped his fingers, turned around, and pulled out a skull. "Not looking anymore. I think I have all the bones I need."

"For what?" But as the words came out of her mouth, she knew the answer. "You're going to make a golem out of bones?"

"I wish I didn't have to. This is a very dangerous, very bad idea. But Sister Claudia is planning on coming back. And she won't be any friendlier than she was before."

Roni moved towards the pile of bones. Cobwebs clinging to them turned her stomach. "Why exactly is this a bad idea? Besides being disgusting."

As Sully set out the bones on the ground in the shape of a person, he said, "Normally when I make a golem, I am taking inanimate objects — like clay or paper or wood — and I bring them to life. These bones once belonged to a living human being. They had been alive already. Bringing once-living things back in this way is not right. Once-living things cling to their will. Which makes them difficult to control. However, these bones are more than simply old. They're ancient. My hope is that they have been dead long enough to no longer care about what they once were."

"And if they do?"

"Then I may be creating more problems than I'm solving. But we can't sit here and wait to be tossed in the rift, can we? If you have a better idea for dealing with these creatures that have taken control of the nuns, let me hear it."

Roni gave it a moment. Then she leaned next to Sully. "How can I help?"

CHAPTER 16

Scavenging ragged bits of cloth, dried rope belts, and even a length of rosary beads, Sully gathered all he needed to tie the bones together. He asked Roni for paper and something to write with. She told him to get started putting the bones in place and she would return with his request. Though it took her several attempts, she eventually located the study of Sister Agnes — a few more times skulking around the tombs and Roni figured she would know the way to the study by heart. On the Sister's desk, Roni grabbed some paper and an old piece of charcoal for writing.

When she returned and saw what Sully had done, she surpassed her initial revulsion and landed right in horrified disgust. With the limited bones available, Sully had not created skeletons that mimicked the human form perfectly. Rather, he had slopped together bones wherever he could tie them to form a humanoid-shaped skeletal structure. He had two of the vile beings set out on the floor — both with legs and arms connected to a spine, but lacking ribs and other bones. Neither had hands and one had femurs for its forearms. Both had skulls — neither with the jawbone —

and Roni would soon learn that those skulls were the most important part of the whole thing.

"Yes, yes," Sully said taking the paper and charcoal. "This will work fine."

Crouching on his hands and knees, he flattened the paper on the hard ground. With the charcoal, he wrote several phrases in Hebrew. Then he rolled each paper into a tight tube and thread one tube into each skull via the eye sockets.

Roni had seen this before — not with human bones but with other objects. All that remained was for Sully to whisper his special words and the creatures would come to life. As long as the paper remained part of the golem, it would stay intact and obey the written commands. That was the real purpose of the skulls. Without them, Sully had no secure place to leave the paper.

As he returned to his feet, the clicks and snaps of his bones made him sound like a third skeleton. "Now, we wait."

"Shouldn't you bring them to life?"

Sully pushed his glasses up his nose. "Do you want to hang out with two living skeletons? I don't. Plenty of time to animate them later."

They did not wait for long. Less than ten minutes and they heard the door at the top of the stairs being unlocked.

Sully hurried over to his skeletons and whispered into the skull of each one. When he finished, he waved Roni away. "Go, go. We must hide."

They scurried around the corner and looked back. They could spy on what happened with ease and the dark shadows would protect them from instant notice. Of course, if the nuns brought a flashlight, the hiding place would be revealed, but that did not concern them. Sully had made it clear — once the skeletons moved in on the nuns and distracted them, he and Roni would dash for the stairs and escape.

As the door opened above, the skeletons twitched. Two nuns climbed down, and the skeletons rose. The one on the left had been tied together using most of the cloth remnants Sully had found. Roni named it Rags. The other skeleton had two femurs in place of its right arm. *Femur Fred,* Roni thought, but then reduced it to simply Fred.

They were hideous creatures, lacking the elegance of many of Sully's golems and even the simple pragmatism of his more hurried creations. These abominations carried with them the sense of dust and fear Sully had during their formation.

The skeletons stood off to the side of the stairs, waiting for the nuns. Before Sister Rachel and Sister Susan reached the bottom, Roni glimpsed the cocky grins on their faces.

"Oh, sweet Roni, I hate to be the one that tell you this," Sister Rachel said, savoring every word. "It looks like Sister Mary agrees that it would be a good idea to try splitting that little girl out of you. We've never done anything like this before, though, so it might kill you."

Sister Susan giggled. "Don't worry. It won't be that bad. Probably. We are still servants of the Lord, and He would not want your deaths on our hands, if it can be avoided."

With the door above left open, dim light made it easier to see. When the nuns reached the bottom, Sister Rachel's face dropped. Sister Susan yelped as her eyes fell upon the living remnants of the Abbey's ancestry.

Roni watched as the skeletons moved on the nuns. She had expected some hissing or groaning sound, some kind of monstrous utterance, but the creatures had no vocal cords, no throats, no tongues, no mouths. Only the sound of their bones tapping against the stone flooring and against each other could be heard.

Sister Susan dropped to her knees, crossed herself, and prayed. Rags lumbered up to her and smacked her on the side of the head. Sister Rachel stumbled backwards from Fred's approach.

"The Parallel Society is a bunch of soulless witches," Sister Rachel said, her words spitting up on Fred's bones. "You hear me? Roni? Old man? I know you're watching. You are servants of the Devil, and I pray that the full wrath of the Lord falls upon your heads."

Sister Susan managed to get to her feet, and she shoved Rags backward. She then turned upon Fred, clasped his spine, and yanked him away from Sister Rachel by putting her weight into swinging him back.

Through angry tears, she said, "Are you all right?"

Sister Rachel scowled. "I'll be fine. Let's go."

"But what about Roni and Sully? We can't leave them here."

Sister Rachel's eyes narrowed, and Roni thought the young woman looked through Sister Susan straight to the corner. "They are responsible for making these abominations. They can suffer with them."

With all of this transpiring in front of the stairs, Roni and Sully never had a chance to escape. That gave Roni the time to wonder why Sister Susan acted like a frightened, meek child. Why did they not use their rifter strength? Why did they not float into the air and fight back? Sister Rachel's arm most likely still hurt, but Sister Susan would have no trouble.

"She's fighting it," Roni whispered. After all, Maria had limited control over Roni, but it felt like something she actively worked at, something Roni resisted. It stood to reason that Sister Susan might not be willing to give up complete control to the rifter inside her.

Having regrouped, Fred and Rags approached for

another assault. The Sisters faced the skeletons.

Sully tapped Roni's shoulder. "Be ready. I think we might get our chance."

Rags stumbled forward and Sister Rachel had little trouble shoving him to the ground — though she winced at her sore shoulder. Fred swung his club-like arm and connected with Sister Susan's hip. She cried out, jostled to the side. Sister Rachel stepped in, took hold of Fred's clavicle and spun him off.

"Why are you taking that?" Sister Rachel said. Confirming Roni's thoughts, she watched as Sister Rachel slapped Sister Susan across the face. "You have been given the greatest gift a nun could ask for. An Angel is inside of you yet you do not allow it to reign free."

"I am not a slave," Sister Susan said. "I will help the Angels. I want to serve them. But I will not have them make me do things I have vowed not to do. You forget — there are rules to our faith."

"They're Angels. They made the rules."

"Why would an Angel encourage me to destroy and kill?"

Rags had managed to get back standing. Fred had turned around enough that it could focus on Sister Susan once again.

Sister Rachel's eyes flashed green. "I thought you were one of us." She shoved Sister Susan into the skeletons.

"No," Sully shouted as he stepped forward.

It was too late. For all their slow movement, once the skeletons had latched onto Sister Susan, they showed no mercy. They sank their top rows of teeth into her neck and shoulder. They fell upon her with more weight than she expected. And if the rifter within her attempted to fight back, Sister Susan fought harder to remain in control — even at the loss of her life.

That was the kind of faith Roni never understood.

"Shalom, shalom," Sully called out — a command word he had written to force the skeletons into disassembling. As their bones clattered to the floor, nothing more than piles of ancient debris, Sister Susan's blood pulsed through her neck. There was no saving her.

Purple-back smoke drifted from Sister Susan's mouth in gentle tendrils. They snaked around each other until they formed a smoke ball. Then the creature floated up the stairwell and disappeared from view.

Sister Rachel nudged Sister Susan's lifeless leg. "Well, Old Man, look what you've done now."

Despite the obvious state of Sister Susan's body, Sully scampered around toward her head to check if there was any chance to resuscitate her. "I thought you were merely fanatical, but now I see, you are crazy."

Sister Rachel let loose a hefty laugh. "No more than you. We both go around trying to save the world. I just happen to be on the right side of things."

Sully inched backwards. Roni wanted to step out of the shadows and warn him that he headed toward a dead end. She stopped. He had to know — he had spent the last hour sifting through every one of the alcoves for the bones he wanted.

Sister Rachel moved closer toward him. "I had thought Sister Susan's ambitions would have been enough. It certainly has been enough for Sister Claudia. But Sister Susan's faith kept getting in the way."

"Not the kind of faith you wanted?"

Moving even further down the dark aisle, Sister Rachel said, "You are awfully brave when you think your friends are coming to save you. But just like in the dorm with your fake magic circle, nobody is coming to help you this time."

In a flash, Roni understood what Sully had been doing.

He had set up the perfect positioning. Sister Rachel had her back to Roni and had gone far enough down the aisle that Roni had access to a weapon. As quietly as possible, Roni crept down the aisle. She crouched and snatched up the largest bone she could find — it wasn't hard. Bones were everywhere.

Ignoring her racing pulse, Roni rushed forward and swung the large bone against the back of Sister Rachel's head. The nun never had a chance. Her body shivered upon contact and slumped to the floor.

Gasping, Roni asked Sully, "Are you okay?"

He emerged from the dark. "I don't shake that easily. Well, not often." He looked at the two nuns on the floor and the piles of bones. "What a shame."

Roni took his hand. "Let's get out of here."

"No." He pulled back. "You go ahead. Go find Gram and Elliot. I'll take care of this mess down here."

Roni wanted to argue, but Sully's tone could not be mistaken. He had issued an order.

"On my way," she said as she climbed the stairs two at a time.

CHAPTER 17

Roni tore into the open air, her mind racing as fast as her heart. She had just seen a nun die. She had just clocked another nun across the back of the head with yet another nun's bones. Being an atheist did not stop her from fearing the bad karma that might come along with these actions.

As she sprinted across the front lawn of the church, headed toward the dorms, she stuttered to a halt. Even if Elliot had managed to get Gram out of the church, they would have found the dorms empty — at least, empty of Roni and Sully. They may have encountered the nuns or they may have escaped and were hiding. If the latter, they could be anywhere in the woods. The cars were still parked outside, so Roni knew they couldn't have gotten too far.

But hiding did not sound like Gram. Especially in her current state of mind. No. Roni suspected Gram and Elliot went on the offensive — not at the nuns directly, but possibly at the rift.

Wishing she had a decent weapon, Roni approached the front of the church. At her gentle push, the door creaked open — she could not recall it having done so in the past — and she entered. The lights leading to the nave were off, but the firelight glow of the rift rose in the stairwell to the right. Softly, Roni descended the spiral staircase.

Halfway down, she heard the chanting — a steady rhythm that lacked musicality but made up for it with fervor. Her legs trembled but she continued on. At the bottom, what she saw made part of her want to race up the stairs, rev up the car, get to an airport, and leave Ireland forever. The other part of her had no choice but to stay and see this through. Gram and Elliot depended on it.

In the center of the room, the rift continued to flow, it's flashing red and orange swirls brightening at irregular intervals. The books that the Parallel Society had been able to salvage surrounded the rift. Five of them — each chained tightly to a bookstand, and each stand chained tightly to each other. The chains zigzagged and crossed one another like the moorings of a complicated tent.

Deeper into the room, near the back corner, Elliot stood with his cane planted firmly on the floor. A dome with a green-yellow hue surrounded the area. At his side, Gram sat on the floor with her right leg out straight. A long gash bled through her pants. As she nursed her leg, she glowered ahead. Two purple-black balls of smoke pressed against the dome.

Any relief Roni could have felt at seeing Elliot protecting Gram washed away under the sound of that chanting. Sister Mary and Sister Claudia prostrated before the rift. Lifting their hands and voices, they chanted foreign words that resembled no language Roni had ever heard. They lowered their heads to the ground and back up again, over and over, chanting the entire time.

With a bright pulse of red from the rift, another smoky creature emerged. It drifted across the room to join the others attempting to break through Elliot's protective bubble.

Roni's shoe scuffed the stone floor. A soft sound, really, but dissonant enough to cut through the chanting. Sister Mary paused and glanced back. Her emerald eyes flared and a mischievous grin formed. She resumed her chanting but not before whispering something to Sister Claudia.

"Run Roni!" Gram crawled toward the edge of the dome. "Get out of here!"

Sister Claudia stood, turned, and sauntered toward Roni. "I'm sorry to see you here alone. I'm guessing Sister Susan and Sister Rachel are not in good shape. I hope you haven't committed any sins. The angels will not like that."

Roni had no interest in trading quips. She had no interest in being polite, either. After all, if Sister Claudia was right, if the rifters were really angels from Heaven, then Roni's soul was doomed to Hell anyway. Might as well go in whole hog.

She stepped forward, clenched her fist, and decked Sister Claudia in the jaw. The surprise on the nun's face made the pain in Roni's hand worthwhile.

Rubbing blood from the corner of her mouth, Sister Claudia snarled. "Bitch."

"Watch the language. There are angels present."

"You'll rot in Hell." Sister Claudia charged forward with her arms up and her fingers splayed out into claws. Her eyes turned green as her feet left the ground. Roni watched her approach and punched again, but Sister Claudia had prepared for it this time. She took the blow in the side while her claws dug into Roni's shoulders. Roni yelled, and Sister Claudia tossed her against the stairs.

As Sister Claudia's feet returned to the ground, she smirked. "Maybe I'll start with breaking both of your legs. You'll cause less trouble that way."

Ignoring the bruised pains running along her back, Roni waited for the nun to be nearly upon her. Then she shot forward. She buried her shoulder into Sister Claudia's gut. The pleasure of hearing Sister Claudia's air knocking from her lungs only matched the satisfaction of tackling the nun to the floor. Roni straddled the woman, made a fist again, and pounded Sister Claudia's chest.

But as the thought hit Roni that she really needed to learn good fighting technique, the Sister bucked her off. In a flash of movement that Roni did not comprehend, Sister Claudia ended up behind her. Somehow the nun had locked one of Roni's arms against her back. She could not move without pulling the arm from the socket or breaking a bone. Pain rifled through her shoulders.

"Perhaps you'd like to feel what you did to Sister Rachel." Sister Claudia tightened her grip and Roni's shoulders burned. "Maybe I'll dislocate both arms just for the fun of it."

Bending back, Sister Claudia lifted off the floor. Roni screamed and her anguish echoed back off the stone walls. Despite the pain and the growing panic, Roni heard Sister Mary continue her chanting. She saw another purple-black ball of smoke emerge from the rift and join the attack on Gram and Elliot. Even as she kicked and thrashed, even as she recognized that she could not break free, she managed to lock eyes with Gram.

She reached towards her grandmother, stretching forward despite the pain. Gram's face dropped — scared and scarred. Roni had mimicked Maria's trapped expression. Whether she had done so of her own volition or because the being inside of her had seen her mother, Roni did not know. But it made all the difference.

Over the years, Roni had seen Gram angry plenty of times. She knew Gram's stern face, her disappointed face, her face that promised a spanking, her face that promised a grounding, and even her face of utter bewilderment. Never before had Roni seen the pure fury that contorted Gram's face at that moment. Despite the pain in her injured leg, Gram positioned herself as upright as possible. A chain lowered from her sleeve.

With a practiced motion, Gram whipped the chain out. It sliced through the dome and lassoed around Sister Claudia's ankle. A swift yank and Sister Claudia spun in the air. Her shocked yelp followed as she tumbled to the ground. Roni rolled sideways.

With her coif pulled back and her wimple askew, Sister Claudia's face twisted like a rabid dog. On all fours she galloped toward Roni. Without time to stand, Roni scooted backwards. She had no weapons. She barely had breath after being held so tight.

Gram wrenched the chain back again. Sister Claudia's eyes widened in shock as she scratched into the floor to no avail. She rolled on her back and grabbed the chain around her ankle. Pulling with great strength, Sister Claudia attempted to free the chain from Gram.

Roni scrambled to her feet. She rushed over and slammed her arms around Sister Claudia's head. She did not know how to perform a proper sleeper hold, but she had seen plenty of them in the movies. Even if it didn't work, her clumsy maneuver would help Gram — perhaps simply buying a little time. At least, Roni hoped so.

Between Gram's chain pulling hard on Sister Claudia's ankle, and Roni tightening her grip around the nun's throat, there was an instant where it seemed they had the advantage. But Roni had forgotten about Sister Mary.

The old nun stood with her arms stretched out and her head arched back. The burning glow of the rift reflected on her white wimple like a lion's mane framing her face. As Roni and Gram struggled with Sister Claudia, Sister Mary walked forward toward the rift.

Roni had seen this before with Sister Ashley. However, this time, the nun approaching did not have the cultish look in her eye of one about to sacrifice herself. Rather, Sister Mary appeared in total control.

When she reached the circle of books and chains, Sister Mary paused. "I hear you, dear angels. I hear you and I welcome you."

With green veins pulsing along the edges of her face and emerald eyes full and bright, Sister Mary took hold of the nearest chain and ripped it loose from the books.

Roni had enough time to catch Gram's terrified gaze. She wanted to say something, but only had a half-second to think a simple summation — *Oh shit.*

CHAPTER 18

An orange wave pulsed out of the rift. Roni braced herself, expecting time to slow and sound to cease. But the light dissipated like water soaked up into a sponge. Sister Mary, Sister Claudia, and Roni exchanged confused gazes.

A distant sound grew like the winding up of a helicopter blade. *Thrum thrum thrum.* As the sound grew louder, it bounced off the walls doubling the noise.

Continuing her steady rhythmic chanting, Sister Mary said, "I am here. Your vessel. Hear my voice. Let it be your lighthouse."

Another orange wave pulsed. Roni could not help but flinch. This time, however, four smokeball creatures shot out of the rift, each one making that strong *thrum* as they broke into this universe.

The creatures pivoted in the air and went straight for Elliot's protection dome. As Roni watched the maneuver, her eyes were drawn away by a dark spot forming in the middle of the rift. The spot did not move with the cloudy swirls of the rift. Instead it grew. It was a black, smoky thing — with touches of purple.

As the helicopter thrumming continued, Roni's stomach

sank. Sister Mary broke into ecstatic laughter.

Roni put it all together — the smoke, the thrumming, the emergence of those creatures — and she took one step toward Gram. Sister Claudia latched onto Roni's arm and held her back. In that same moment, the creatures busted through.

Thrum thrum thrum. Each sound spat a new smoke creature from the rift. They shot out like bullets machine-gunning through the air.

Roni dropped to the floor, taking Sister Claudia with her. The rifters rattled overhead as they kept coming in a steady stream of purple-black smoke. The roar of their entrance rivaled any giant machine mankind had made. Sifting through the rhythmic crescendo, Roni could hear Sister Mary's gleeful cries.

Something metal wrapped around Roni's wrist — Gram's chain. She glanced up and snatched a peak. Her grandmother's face betrayed the desperation in her heart. Roni scrambled across the floor, but Sister Claudia latched to her foot.

Roni tried to kick loose. The nun's grip was tight. She flashed a vicious grin promising never to let go. Gram pulled harder on the chain. Roni wondered if Gram might do Sister Claudia's work for her — dislocate Roni's arm and cause serious injury.

Sister Claudia repositioned her legs to give her more leverage. "Open your mouth. Let the Angels in."

As she leaned back, the strain on Roni's leg worsened. One of these two women would soon rip Roni apart.

Not going to happen, Roni thought.

She let go of the chain. The sudden change in force sent Sister Claudia tumbling backward. Roni hit the floor hard on her tailbone and cried out. She rolled onto her stomach, popped to her knees, and raced across the floor. She could hear Sister Claudia growling as the nun recovered. The air had become thick with purple-black smoke, and Roni feared breathing in too deeply. Up ahead, she saw Gram's chain.

Just a few feet.

"I'm going to destroy you," Sister Claudia said, her voice louder, closer, more animalistic than Roni dared imagine.

Roni had the urge to glance back, to see if her ears misjudged the distance, but she kept her focus on that chain. So close.

Something touched her — a finger grazing her back. Roni vaulted forward. Her hand grabbed the end of the chain and she rolled up upon it like a scroll trying to tie itself. "Now, Gram! Now!"

The chain snapped taut and zipped against the ground as Gram pulled hard. Like a flapping fish, Roni tumbled as Gram reeled her in toward the protection of Elliot's dome. The chain spun Roni around. Skidding on her back, ignoring the burn of her tearing skin, she saw Sister Claudia stand full upright. The nun sprinted after her with a face glowing with green anger.

Roni passed through into the dome, and all the rage of Sister Claudia, all the maniacal chanting of Sister Mary, all the jackhammering *thrums* of the rifters pouring into the room — all of it muted. Roni heard her own hard breathing and little more. She felt the fire in her shoulder and the pulsing aches in her hips. Sweat covered her body, stinging her lips with saltiness.

As Gram spooled her chain up her sleeve, Roni crawled over and hugged the old woman. Gram did not hesitate to return the touch. Roni pressed her face into her grandmother's safe bosom and the strength of Gram's arms around her found the right amount of pressure to exert. The embrace lasted only seconds but it would take two libraries full of books to express it in words between them.

"Look," Gram whispered.

Roni followed her gaze. Sister Mary and Sister Claudia crouched on the floor, their arms around each other. They no longer looked joyous or ecstatic or even maniacal. They looked alarmed.

Both had bruises on their faces. Sister Mary's right cheek bled from an open gash. Sister Claudia's tunic had been torn. Tears wet her cheeks.

"How have we failed you?" Sister Mary cried out.

"Please, forgive us." Sister Claudia covered her face and lowered her head.

Roni tightened her grip on Gram's arm. "Can you save them?"

Gram shook her head. "They have those creatures inside them. The dome filters out all bio-signatures but ours. If we permit them into the dome, we will let the creature's biological signature in as well. The dome won't work for us anymore. All those things will flood in here." Gram clutched the crucifix around her neck. "I will send my prayers for them."

Roni held back shouting that she had Maria inside her. Since the dome continued to work, Maria could not be one of the rifters. But she knew the argument already — Maria, whatever she was, came partially from the real Maria. Of course, she wasn't a rifter. Of course, the dome would hold.

Without warning, a swarm of rifters paused in the air. Using that same silent communication Roni had seen before, they turned toward the nuns. Though the creatures lacked eyes or mouths or any visible sign of a face, Roni swore they looked upon the Sisters with malevolent glee.

They attacked.

Like angry wasps, the creatures dove in on the nuns. Sister Mary gyrated as one hit after another pummeled her body. Sister Claudia remained prone on the ground, shuddering under the endless attacks. The screams of both nuns vibrated through the air as their flesh tore from their bodies. Blood splashed into the air but the swarm of purple-black smoke soaked it up before it could return to the floor. Their cries worsened as their muscles tore. Soon though, they lacked throats with which to make any sound. Seconds later, bones and glistening flesh were all that remained of the two women.

Watching as the smoke creatures changed course to pile up against the dome, Roni turned towards Gram. "Now what do we do?"

Though safe for the moment, Roni understood that soon the dome would crumble. Elliot had lowered his forehead to his cane — all his strength and concentration poured into keeping that dome together. But the air glowed purple from the mass of the creatures surrounding them. The numerous rifters blocked out the sunlight. They had become a brick wall made of purple-black smoke, and soon Elliot's strength would fail.

"I am so sorry, ladies," he said, his voice weak and strained. "I can only hold on a little longer."

Roni watched the creatures pushing against each other, writhing in their attempts to break through. She imagined the pain that would come. She did not want to die, of course. But most of all, she did not want to die the way the nuns had.

A crack formed halfway up the dome. While Roni knew the dome had been made only of energy, that there was no glass or solid surface of any kind to actually crack, Elliot's weakening condition manifested in this manner. Or perhaps she was wrong — she had limited knowledge about the Parallel Society. Perhaps the dome he had created this time actually was made of a solid substance. After all, she could hear the cracking as she watched the splits spider outward in different directions.

Wisps of purplish smoke seeped through. Roni and Gram skirted backward, pressing up against one of the two stone walls making the corner. When Elliot's hand slipped down his cane, the crack widened — still not large enough for an entire rifter to slip through, but plenty of their probing, smoky tendrils found ways in.

Gram put her arm around Roni's shoulder and clasped her head with the other hand. She pulled Roni's face down to her breast and held her tight. "I'm sorry for all you've had to suffer through. Your mother and father had so many secrets, and it was never fair for you to be burdened with that mystery. I'm sorry you never got to understand about your lost time. I can only offer you my arms and my prayers. I hope the Lord can forgive us all our trespasses and I pray we shall be sent to His loving bosom."

Under any other circumstance, Roni would have been offended by Gram's words. But here, as Elliot dropped to his knees and the dome ripped into pieces, she found Gram's warmth comforting.

A storm of rifters slammed downward into the dome.

A loud bang like modern demolition.

Roni's head popped up in time to see the wall next to her break open. The stones shot outward, thrusting the smoke creatures aside. A large stone golem ducked its way in. Sully stood at the open hole in the wall.

"Care for a little help?" he asked.

CHAPTER 19

Sully's golem had dug a steep incline from the surface down toward the basement wall. With Gram using Roni as a crutch, the two managed to muddle their way to the top. Sully and his golem came out next. Elliot emerged last with his cane held chest-high and pointed at the wall — keeping the remnants of his protective dome together.

"It's okay," Sully said. "They won't come out."

Though clearly skeptical, Elliot let the head of his cane fall to the ground. Several of the rifters drifted outside, but they merely floated up the wall to enter the church again through a stained-glass window. Like dogs reacting to an invisible fence, they refused to cross further out.

As Elliot climbed up the dirt and rocks, he said, "How did you know they can't follow us?"

"They can, but they won't. When I was scavenging stones to build the golem, I noticed that nothing was coming outside. And I never saw the one creature that left Sister Susan's body roaming the grounds. I assumed it came back in here."

"Assumed? So you didn't really know?"

Sully shrugged. "I made an educated guess."

With gravelly impatience, Gram said, "The two of you can bicker later. We need to find some place to regroup. And my leg is killing me."

"Agreed," Sully said. "We can take the cars and drive off, but I don't like the idea of leaving this rift unattended. Especially now."

"You're right. The time it would take us to drive to a nearby town might be the time it takes for this rift to decimate all of Ireland."

Roni gestured with her chin. "What about the dorm?"

Sully stepped forward, turned around, and eyed the various buildings. "Presumably, at some point, those creatures will come out of that church. Since they appear to have some type of telepathy between each other, we have to assume all the new creatures will have learned what the older ones know — I would not want to go to the dorm or the library. They would be too familiar with those areas already."

"Where then?" Elliot said, resting against the bumper of the car.

Roni said, "If you follow the path beyond the dorms, there's a barn on the hill. Can all of Ireland survive long enough for that?"

"It'll have to." Sully headed off with the others following behind. "We can rest up and figure out our next move."

Raising her voice, Gram said, "And somebody can tell me, by all that's holy, what is going on around here."

The barn turned out to be smaller than expected but still serviceable. A tractor that could not have been used in nearly five years took up much of the center aisle. Old stalls with rotting wood had been filled with rusted tools, weathered boxes, and whatever else the nuns wanted to discard. A hayloft overlooked them, and Roni's quick search up there suggested they had a good view of the church, if they didn't mind stepping on rat droppings.

As Elliot ran his healing across Gram's leg, Sully found a stack of folding chairs and formed a small circle with them. "I know there's a lot going on between you two ladies," Sully said. "We're out of time. That rift is spewing out living relics. We've got to find a way to put them back in. So, set aside your differences and start talking with each other."

"Roni and I are fine." Gram crossed her arms over her chest.

"Yeah," Roni said. "You didn't see but we hugged it all out."

Sully raised an eyebrow. "One hug and all is well? That must've been one powerful hug."

"It's enough for now," Gram said.

Roni added, "We know how to put our disagreement on hold. Besides, we did have a hug. It happened right before your golem broke down the wall."

Sully had set the golem on sentry duty outside. "Fine. Sister Rachel is tied up underneath the library. I fear what might happen when she gets out and joins the others in the church."

"You left her down there?"

"You'd rather I carry her around or bring her up here?"

"No, but —"

"I wasn't going to kill her. We're not that kind of people."

"I only meant —"

"This is what I'm talking about. Stop criticizing each other, stop questioning each other, and start dealing with the situation as it is. We're running out of time."

Rubbing his forehead, Elliot said, "Perhaps the two of you could explain to Gram and I what is going on, what happened to Sister Rachel, or even Sister Susan, everything. I went to get Gram in the church and found Sister Mary had taken her down to the rift. When I got down there, everything went bad. I barely had enough time to create that protection field."

Pushing his glasses up his nose, Sully said, "It's a bit complicated."

"No, it's not," Roni said. She stood and stretched her arms. After a deep breath, she said, "This is all my fault. It's mine to explain."

"Roni," Sully said, the warning unmistakable.

"Just because you're the leader, doesn't give you the right to withhold from the group."

Gram snickered. "Not so easy, huh?"

Suddenly taking interest in the barn's wood framing, Sully declined to answer.

Before the Old Gang could launch into another bout of bickering, Roni delved in and covered all the details from the moment she and Gram had arrived at the Abbey. Much of it Gram and Elliot had already heard, but Roni wanted to make sure that all members of the team had the same information. When she got to the point where she woke up after releasing Maria, she had the thirst for a strong whiskey. Pressing on, she described the sensations she felt and the voices she heard. And she watched Gram closely. The old woman's face shifted from one emotion to another as if someone controlled her muscles by remote and kept randomly pressing buttons. Roni worried Gram might have a stroke.

Once she finished, Roni perched on the edge of the chair next to Gram. "I don't know if you can believe me, but I didn't do any of this to hurt you. I'm trying to do the right thing. I guess I blew it. I'm sorry."

The barn grew quiet as the team digested Roni's tale. At

length, Gram lifted a shaking, wrinkled hand and placed it on Roni's cheek. She looked over Roni's face as if seeing her granddaughter for the first time. Her shallow eyes welled up and her jowls quivered.

In a shaking voice, Gram said, "My baby? Are you in there?"

The attack came stronger than ever before. All the hairs on Roni's body stood as her skin prickled. The smell of molding hay and damp earth faded — replaced with enough sugar in the air to fill a candy factory. The high-pitched whine became a wolf's howl next to Roni's ear.

She doubled over to the ground, pressing the palms of her hands against her ears. Tears streamed from her eyes, and when she gazed up at Gram, her blurred vision knocked forty years off the woman. She saw a young mother reaching down towards her.

Her jaw acted involuntarily. It locked open as her throat convulsed out a voice that did not belong to her. "Mommy?"

"Baby? Maria? Is that really you?" The hope in Gram's voice rose above the horror in her trembling tone.

"I love you, Mommy. Love you. Miss you."

Gram dropped to her knees. Blubbering through her words, she said, "Oh, my sweet baby, I'm so sorry. I should never have brought you here. I was so cocky back then and look what it caused. The Lord has punished me."

"Please. This time. Let me go."

"I know, I know. I'm so sorry. I should never have let you go with me."

"I have to go. You need me. Stop this."

Roni's throat burned as if she had spent the day throwing up acrid bile. Her jaw closed and she collapsed in a fetal position. She could feel Elliot's large hands resting on her head as he performed his regular miracles —

checking over for any internal injuries and healing her, if necessary. But she did not feel injured — mostly. Used. She felt used. As when she woke in a stranger's bed, her body spent, her regret growing.

She did not regret bringing Maria out of that hell. Despite the pain it had caused them both, she knew she had done the right thing. She had to have.

With Elliot's help, she sat up and eventually made it to one of the folding chairs. Sully returned from outside — checking on his golem and the church, no doubt.

"How long have I been out?" she asked.

"Only a few minutes," Elliot said.

Gram paced the length of the barn, her fingers rolling over the beads of her rosary — she always had one in her pocket at hand — as she mouthed one prayer after another. Sully slouched on one of the folding chairs, leaned his head back, and stared at the ceiling. He looked like a younger man, though Roni worried he might have trouble getting out of that position.

Elliot shifted over to Sully and patted his forehead with a handkerchief. "You must be careful not to exhaust yourself. We cannot afford to lose you. Ever."

Sully reached up and clasped Elliot's hand between his own. "You are the best friend a man could ask for. But you worry too much. I'm not exhausted at all."

"Lying to me will not help."

Sully sat forward, took off his glasses, and rubbed the bridge of his nose. "I said I'm okay."

"I know that look on you. It's not a good one."

Feeling a little stronger, Roni said, "You said it yourself — we don't have time for these kinds of things. Out with it."

Sully's head snapped up. "I think I have an idea for how we might close the rift."

"I thought it couldn't be closed."

"That was before you came along and pulled out Maria. That was before these nuns found a way to call all those creatures loose. Things are different now, more different than any time ever before when concerned with this rift. We can use that to our advantage."

Gram rejoined the group, opting to stand behind her chair. "She has to go back. Doesn't she?"

"I'm afraid so," Sully said, gazing at his hands to avoid looking at anyone else. "I've been thinking about all that we've learned. I believe that back when you were young and Maria was split — back then, the creatures within the rift had found a way to reach out. We know Sister Mary had already been taken over, but the creature inside her had not been able to pull out any others."

"You think they stole my Maria in a failed attempt to break free?"

"And then all these years since, the piece of her trapped in that rift acted like a stopper on a vial. Once Roni broke her free, the vial was open. The way for the others to come out became clearer. They merely needed a guide, and the nuns provided that."

Roni stood too fast and fell back to her chair. "We can't do this. We can't send Maria back into that awful place."

"We don't have a choice. It's our duty to protect this universe — no matter what."

"But if she's only a stopper, then all we'll have succeeded in doing is preventing more of those creatures from coming in. The rift will still be open and there will still be hundreds of those creatures around."

Gram shared a grim look with Elliot. "I'll have to make a special book. One that can vacuum up all those things."

Elliot said, "And I will have to build a dome around the entire church to contain them until your book is ready."

Lifting his head, Sully gazed at his team, and Roni could feel the regret seeping out of each one. "Then it is possible," he said. "We don't have time to do the proper research. Do you think this'll work?"

"I won't do it," Roni said. "This is all that's left of my mother. Of Gram's daughter. We can't just let her go. And after all I've done to get her back."

"It won't be so easy as letting her go." Sully brushed his hands against his pants and stood. "You will have to go, too. As near to the rift as it takes for Maria to be pulled out of you."

Tossing the chair aside, Gram stepped forward, putting herself between Roni and Sully. "Absolutely not."

"They're connected. But if you chain her —"

"She'll still be at risk."

"There will always be risk."

"Then no. Lord knows I am not going to lose the both of them."

Sully gazed off toward the church. "Then we've already lost."

CHAPTER 20

Rain pattered against the roof of the barn. Roni stood in the hayloft, feeling the occasional raindrop splat upon her nose, as she watched the church in the distance. If not for the intensifying purple glow of the rift, she would have had difficulty seeing the church at all. Like picking out the nuns in the night, the dark stone of the church blended in with the stormy sky.

Soon, they would have to do something. Even in the few minutes Roni had spent watching the church, the pulsing glow of the creatures worsened. The rift kept shooting them out, and by morning at the latest, they would be ready to break free. In fact, the only thing stopping the Parallel Society from fighting those creatures right away was that they had no idea what to do.

No, that's not true. Sully had an idea, but Gram refused to let it happen. Roni did, too, for that matter.

Below her, Elliot sat ramrod straight on a folding chair and meditated. Gram had resumed her pacing of the barn and her praying with the rosary. And Sully — he puttered with his golem.

Not only did they lack a viable option of what to do, but

it seemed to Roni that none of them worked hard enough
to secure an answer. Until she heard Gram approach Sully
with a hushed tone that piqued her interest.

"There must be a better way," she said. "We have no
reason to believe your plan will work."

"I'm taking the best educated guess that I can."

"It's still just a guess."

The rain strengthened creating an incessant drumroll on
the barn roof. Forced to speak louder than he had intended,
Sully said, "I'm in charge around here. I don't take this
lightly. But we do have a responsibility to the universe —
sacrifice comes with that."

Roni stepped back from the lip of the hayloft and
plopped down on a bale that looked reasonably unused by
rats.

Maybe Sully was right. Maybe she would have to accept
that sacrificing her life was part of her duty. After all, if she
refused to help, she sentenced so many others to a horrible
fate — perhaps the entire world. Was her puny life worth
more than all the billions of the world? Besides, all this
trouble existed because of her mistake. If she had listened
to Gram and left the rift alone, none of this would have
happened. The nuns would still be wishing for somebody
to come along who could use the book Sister Agnes had
stolen long ago. The rift would still be a stabilized anomaly.
And Maria would have remained locked away.

"I don't know if you can hear me," she whispered to the
empty air. "I don't even know if I want you to hear me. No,
that's not true. I do want that. Part of me wants to call you
Mom and feel your arms around me. Part of me thinks I'm
like your big sister and that I should have my arms around
you. I don't know what to think about any of this. But I
want you to know why I did it. Even if the Old Gang never
understands, even if you don't, I think I should at least try

to give you that much."

The skin on the back of her neck prickled which she took to be the closest thing she could get for communication.

"I don't have a lot of memories of you — that is, the you that grew up into an adult and gave birth to me. There was the car accident. That I remember — but really only the aftermath. The moment when Gram told me what had happened and what would become of me. That sort of thing. Even that is a fuzzy haze. I don't know how many weeks I walked around like a zombie waiting for it all not to be true. But it was. You had died and my father went a bit nuts and I lost a lot of what I knew. But I do have a few rare, precious memories of you. Growing up, when it came to talking about you, Gram tended to focus on all the trouble you got into, but you weren't all bad. In fact, you could be sweet and lovely."

Roni closed her eyes and swam through the dark emptiness of her memories. What she summoned up, she could see as clearly as if it had happened only minutes ago — not too difficult considering the few memories of her mother that she had. With such a limited library at her disposal, she had visited this memory an inordinate amount of times.

She was a girl, around ten, and she had woken from a nightmare. The clock read 3:24 am, and she knew her father would not be around. He had been stuck working the graveyard shift at a twenty-four hour diner. He was the one she preferred to go to when upset, but she needed some comfort regardless. Roni no longer recalled the nightmare itself, but she could still feel how unsettling the dream had been for her, the way it left her skin sensitive to the rub of the sheets, the way the night's quiet caused her heart to beat faster, the way she could taste the danger lurking in her sub-conscious — waiting for her to sleep again so that it could take over.

They were living in a two-bedroom apartment more suited for college students than a young family. From her bedroom doorway, she spotted the light on in the kitchen. As she approached, she heard her mother sniffle and whimper.

Roni never found out what had upset her mother, or if she had, that part of the memory was lost, too. The instant Maria spotted little Roni approaching, she wiped away her tears, blew her nose, and wriggled out a smile for her daughter.

"Did I wake you?" she asked.

The sound of her voice echoed in Roni's head. She had heard those four words so many times that they began to lose all meaning. Whenever in her life she felt the need for her mother's love, she turned to this memory. The fact that her mother could have been so upset about something yet drop it simply to offer concern for her daughter's nightmare always left adult-Roni in a state of awe.

"I wish I could show you more," she said to the hayloft. "That's the best one I have. I just wanted you to not think so terribly of your other half."

Roni's skin flushed with warmth, and she thought it would end there. A simple, straightforward response — she needed no more. But the warmth continued and the temperature increased. It did not become painful, but Roni broke out into a sweat. Her eyes closed. And Maria shared her own memory.

Transported into the rift, Roni swam in a thick soup of orange and red and yellow smoke. No surfaces around her. No up or down. As if she hovered in the middle of the ocean, unsure which way led to the surface.

Most sounds had diminished to the point of being

inaudible. Movement slowed, too. Not as bad as when the rift had sent pulses through Roni, but bad enough.

She wanted to move her hand, but of course, this was not her hand to move. It belonged to Maria. This was the girl's memory.

And in that memory, Maria showed a moment when she managed to jerk her body fast to the side. The bright fog of orange reacted equally fast — as if she and the smoke sat upon a seesaw. If she moved one way, the smoke mirrored in the opposite direction. Always matching her speed. It took a long time — possibly years, Maria could not be sure how time progressed in there — but she came to see that her presence in the rift let her control it ... to an extent.

"You really do stabilize that thing," Roni whispered.

Maria offered one last touch — not an image but a sensation. A vengeful wrath overcame Roni, a desire to protect through destruction, to tear down the object of Maria's trauma, of her torture.

She jolted to her feet. Her pulse pounded hard enough to move the skin on her chest. Leaping for the ladder, she hurried down to the barn floor. Gasping, she said, "I know what we have to do."

The Old Gang snapped their attention towards her, each one moving in close to listen.

"We were right that Maria had stabilized the rift. But we don't want her to go back there to stabilize it again. That would not solve any of our current problems, and it would be cruel to her. But she's made it known to me what to do."

Gram braced herself on Sully's arm. "She's going to sacrifice herself. Isn't she?"

"It's painful in there. She doesn't want to go back to that. And she knows she can't stay with us here."

Sully said, "But if we don't send her back, how can she

stabilize the rift?"

"She's not going to stabilize it. She's going to overload it. She's going to destroy it." To Elliot, Roni asked, "Can you do anything to help with that?"

Elliot picked up his cane. "I can amplify her energy, but it'll go off in all directions like a bomb. We've had books around that thing for centuries — each one pushing its energy into the rift and that's barely contained the thing. If we can't focus Maria's power right into the rift, it won't have a serious impact."

"Roni is still connected to Maria," Sully said. "She could direct the energy — then that would not be a problem."

"Like what we did in that little town in France about thirty years ago."

"Exactly. Although back then, you sent your energy through the town square like a magnifying glass. We won't have that for Maria's energy."

Straightening, Gram clutched her crucifix. "We have something better. We have the Lord's church itself."

The men paused to share a look with her.

Clearing her throat, Roni said, "The only problem I see in this is how do we get her in a position so that her energy can be amplified into the church and then into the rift?"

Sully's face took an ominous turn. "You forget — the two of you are connected."

"Trust me, I haven't forgotten."

"Then, you do understand what that means, yes? Using the church like you suggest?"

"If we use the church itself, I'm guessing that means from somewhere in the building?"

Gram approached Roni and pulled her in for a hug. "Oh dear, it's worse than that. You have to go into the center of the rift."

Roni pictured the rift tearing apart Sister Ashley, Sister

Claudia, and Sister Mary. "Oh."

Waving his hands, Sully shook his head and mumbled as he walked the length of the barn. He chuckled and clicked his tongue. Then he pointed at his golem. "Don't worry. I know exactly what to do." Gram raised an eyebrow, and Sully shrunk a bit. "Well, almost exactly. I got a good idea. Trust me."

CHAPTER 21

Roni leaned against the open barn doors and watched the rain soaking the ground. Behind her, Sully had dismantled his stone golem. With Elliot's help, the two men made preparations for Sully's plan.

"It's going to be okay," Gram said as she sidled up.

"Sure." Roni kept her eyes on puddles forming on the ground. "You almost sound convincing."

Gram stayed silent for a moment. When she leaned against the other side of the barn door, she said, "There's always danger when you come out into the field. Always risks."

"Not so much in the library, huh?"

"There's eyestrain."

Roni laughed. "I'll be okay. I mean I'm scared shitless, but —"

"Watch the language."

"But I'll do the job."

Gram pressed the tips of her fingers together. "If there were another way."

"I know. I agree. We don't have time to hit the books."

"Be sure. You've seen me all over the map with this. It's

hard to know what's right. This isn't even my first time in a terrible situation and it's still hard. It's okay if you've changed your mind."

Roni breathed in the fresh, wet air. "I appreciate that, but it's not necessary. An hour ago, I would've thought different. But I had a conversation — of sorts — with Maria." She frowned as the words to articulate her thoughts evaded her. At length, she said, "It's time I move forward. The past won't go anywhere. I'll figure it out when I need to. But the world needs the Parallel Society now. Right?"

Gram gazed down at her hands. "Very brave." She pulled out her rosary and wrapped it around her hand. "I wonder if you might do me a favor before you go over to the boys."

"Of course."

"Maybe I could talk with Maria?"

Roni choked back the crack in her voice. "She doesn't really talk."

"She did before. She used your voice."

"And that hurt like … heck. I'm not sure she could do that again, anyway. I got the sense that it took a lot of effort. But she can hear you. Say what you want to say. I'll let you know how she responds."

Holding her rosary so tight that her fingers turned white, Gram stepped over towards Roni. She inclined her head close enough that she would not have to raise her voice to be heard. "I don't know what you are. My daughter? Part of her? Maybe just an echo of her being used by some creature in another universe. So many nights I prayed for the Lord to give me the means with which to help you. I always thought that meant bringing you home, making you whole.

"Earlier, I was in the church praying, and I saw how hard I had been on you. Not this side of you, but the other you — the one I raised into a young woman. So much of her rebellion came because of how hard I was. I think now I blamed her partially for surviving. I think I also blamed myself for taking you here to begin with, taking you to die.

"And now, I'm sending you to die again.

"I don't know if this matters to you, but I want you to know that I've done all I could for Roni. I've tried to make up for my failings. I've tried to make her into a woman that you could be proud of. I've tried…"

Gram lifted her head, and her glistening eyes held with Roni's. A soft utterance escaped her throat before she hurried off to one of the horse stalls. She crouched down, and though Roni tried to give the woman her privacy, there was no mistaking the sound of weeping.

Elliot walked up and put his arm on Roni's shoulder. "Come on. We are ready. Let your grandmother have a moment alone."

He escorted Roni back into the center of the barn. There she saw the rocks had been laid out according to size. Several small rocks had been placed shoulder-width apart on the ground, roughly in the shape of footprints.

Sully gestured to these footprint rocks. "Stand on them, and we can get started."

With all her concentration devoted to keep from shaking, Roni placed one foot on each of the stone forms. Sully and Elliot immediately got to work. With expert care, Sully chose specific rocks and placed them around Roni's feet. Elliot did the same, following Sully's instructions, while periodically giving Roni a reassuring nod.

As the rocks piled higher up the legs, Sully said to Elliot, "Don't worry about the exact shape. When we're ready, it'll work."

Roni did not share his confidence but kept silent. Every rock further up her body brought with it the weight of what they planned to do. Every extra pound pressing against her skin added to her fear.

When they reached her waist and prepared to lock down her arms, Gram rushed forward. "Hold on."

"We've already talked about this," Sully said, putting out his hands like a crossing guard. "We don't have another choice. There just isn't the time."

Pushing him aside, Gram stepped up towards Roni. She grabbed Roni's right hand and wrapped her rosary around the wrist. "I don't care that you are a non-believer. I have faith enough for the both of us. And if that thing in you is really Maria, then she has faith, too."

Roni clenched the rosary beads. Before she could respond, before she could even say a simple *I love you,* Gram turned away. Sully returned with a piece of paper. He placed the paper in her left hand.

"As long as that paper stays together, the golem will stay together. Strong. You can trust me."

As Sully returned to stacking rocks, Elliot paused. He stepped before Roni. "If you wish, I can create a little something that might ease you."

She shook her head. She needed to stay clear and focused. But she could not say those words — she did not trust her voice to hold steady. Elliot kissed her cheek before returning to help Sully.

By the time they reached her neck, she could no longer hold back the tears. Her body wanted to shake, but the tightly packed stones prevented it. She gazed upward, hoping to dry out her eyes — she didn't even have the movement to reach up and rub them. Lightning flashed and thunder crackled above them, and Roni pictured herself as Frankenstein's monster. The tears flowed faster.

"What is this?" A voice scraped as a nun lurched into the barn, her lame foot dragging behind. "Another abomination?" Stepping out of the rain, Sister Rachel wiped her bleeding mouth with the dark sleeve of her torn habit. "The Angels keep coming. You can't stop them. Soon, the world will become a vessel for them all. And I will gladly be the first to cast you demons back to Hell."

From the side, out of the shadows, Gram stepped forth wielding a shovel. She swung hard and slapped the nun in the back of the head. The young woman folded to the floor.

"Poser," Gram said and spit on the ground.

Standing with rocks in his hands, Sully said, "You're a Catholic. You can't go around striking nuns. We could've done that for you."

"You said she was tied up below the library. Does this look tied up to you?"

"I did my best. I didn't have a lot of good rope. I was using rags from over a hundred years ago." Sully slammed two rocks onto Roni's shoulders. "You think it's so easy? Next time, you find a way out of the crypt filled with bones and rats."

"Next time it might be a Rabbi instead of a nun. You saying you'll fight a rabbi?"

"It depends. Is he Orthodox or Reform?"

Roni laughed — a hardy, full-throated laugh. Tears streamed down, her face reddened, and she laughed more. Though Gram and Sully failed to find the humor, Elliot leaned back his head and roared alongside Roni.

At length, Gram said, "Fine, fine. I will tie up this excuse for a nun properly. You boys finish with the rocks. If that's okay, my leader?"

Waving his hand as he returned to work, Sully said, "Tie her up, don't tie her up, do what you think is right. We've got serious work to do."

He stepped back and passed an appraising eye up and down the thick pile of stones that encased Roni. "You ready?"

Roni nodded.

"Elliot and I are going to cover your head now. It might feel tight in there for a while. But once I whisper my commands, you'll be able to breathe fine. Okay?"

With a strong, steady voice, Roni said, "Let's go save the universe."

CHAPTER 22

Sully's whisper could not come fast enough. From the moment he placed the final stone, the one that covered her face, Roni fought back claustrophobic panic. She had never suffered from such a thing before, but then she had never been entombed in a rock pile before. The feeling of being buried alive did not sit well with her. Yet when Sully finally whispered his incantation into the golem's ear, the stones muffled his voice too much for her to catch what he said. Not that she would have understood the Hebrew.

Regardless, the golem came to life. She could feel it breaking out of the stone mound, feel it moving on its own. Though she formed its skeleton, she had no control over its actions. Two small stones rolled off the face so that she could see. A third stone popped out providing her a much-needed breathing hole.

"Relax your muscles," Sully said. "The less resistance you provide, the easier the golem will move, and the less chance of you being injured."

"Injured? You didn't say anything about this thing injuring me."

"I'm saying it now. Relax, and you'll be fine."

Gram watched from several steps back, both fascinated and horrified with what Roni was expected to do. "Good luck," she managed.

As the golem stepped out into the rain, Roni caught a glimpse of Elliot up in the hayloft. He had his cane held above his head, nearly vertical, and his free hand repeating several complex motions. She knew from past experience that much of the magic Elliot created took time. If she reached the church before he was ready, if she enacted her part of the plan too early, she didn't think she would survive. But he promised it would be okay, and she believed him. She had to.

She squeezed both her hands tight — the golem paper in her left, Gram's rosary beads in her right. The golem proceeded down the hill and the rain soaked through its stone crevices fast. Trickles of water fell down Roni's back, chilling her spine and drenching her pants.

Steady footsteps brought the golem closer to the church. Roni tried to follow Sully's instructions, tried to relax her body, but the excruciatingly slow pace only amped up her tension. She closed her eyes — the golem did not need for her to see in order to move — and she attempted to contact Maria.

This failed. Either Maria could no longer communicate or she refused to communicate. Probably the latter. Probably she needed to put her attention into the final moments ahead. They would be, after all, her actual, final moments — if all went as expected.

After fifteen minutes of a walk that should have taken three, Roni and the golem trudged by the dorms. A rich, purple color pulsed through the windows of the church ahead. The building had become so thick with rifters that the stone walls glowed as well. It was as if Prince had come back from the dead to put on his greatest private concert ever — but Roni knew that inside awaited no great music. Inside, awaited death. Hopefully not her own.

Once the golem set its stone foot upon the first stairs leading into the church, two rifters slipped outside and hovered in front of the entranceway. They made no noise. Simply hovered there, dripping smoke onto the ground. The golem halted. This would be the first crucial moment.

Sully had said that the living golem form would cover up any sense of Roni — any sense of her presence. Of course, he had no way to know for sure. He based his guess on the fact that they never noticed the golem when he broke through the stone wall. As the rifters descended around her head and drifted up and down the golem's stone body, she made sure not to move. She closed her eyes. She waited and hoped Sully had been right.

Her nervous breaths bounced off the rock around her. Between her heartbeats they sounded like a howling wind in a heavy storm. Lightning flashed again, brightening her closed eyelids red, and thunder split the sky.

Roni kept expecting a strange sensation from the touch of the rifters. Perhaps an electric tingle or a static rise or even something as simple as pressure like a hand placed on her back. She felt nothing. The only indication that she had succeeded — the golem moved once again.

She fluttered her eyes open as the golem entered the narthex. The doors leading into the nave were wide open, and a weird, blasphemous service took place. Purple-black balls of smoke filled the pews, the walls, the air, all the way to the vaulted ceiling. A curved tunnel cut through the mass of creatures, leading from the nave straight down to the apse like some twisted wedding pathway formed from friends reaching out to each other.

Roni thought that if the nuns had been around to see this, they would have certainly believed it to be the hand of their Lord. To her, she saw the results of the rift beneath the floor. Like magnets moving metal shavings into odd shapes, the energy from the rift forced these creatures into this strange configuration.

Their faceless bodies pivoted and turned, and with each movement, she thought that surely, they would see her now. They would attack full force, rip apart the stone golem protecting her, and then tear her skin from her bones. She could see it as if it had already happened.

Tightening her hand around Gram's rosary, she fought the urge to scream. Her bladder suddenly decided to put pressure on her abdomen. At least that provided her with something else to focus on. No way would she allow her bladder to let loose.

The golem turned to the right and headed for the spiral staircase leading below. Sully believed it would have little problem navigating the narrow stairs — its body was only slightly larger than Roni's. If it could not succeed at the task, it would back up, leave the church, and enter through the hole in the wall made by the previous golem.

"I'd rather use the stairs," Sully had said. "If the creatures do not react to you being inside the stone, I don't want to give any indication of what we are up to. Coming in through the hole which was the site of the previous attack might tip them off. That is, if they think in any logical way."

That was the thing. They had no idea how these creatures thought. The things lacked eyes yet sensed the world around them to some extent. They lacked mouths, they lacked arms, they lacked anything of substance yet had caused devastating harm already.

But Sully's golem-building skills proved their excellence. The golem navigated the spiral staircase with ease, and in moments, Roni found herself standing before the rift.

The orange-red swirls continued in their mesmerizing

fashion, and rifters popped out sporadically. But the rapid-fire force which Roni had witnessed earlier had ceased. Those rifters that did emerge quickly floated upward, seeping through the cracks in the ceiling, to join their brethren in the nave.

For the most part, the basement was empty. Roni knew that would not last for long. Soon, Elliot's magic would take hold and she would have to make her move. But all indications suggested Elliot had yet to accomplish his task. She had to wait — again.

Speaking through shivering breaths, keeping her voice barely audible, she said, "Maria?"

She counted to ten, hoping to feel an answer. Nothing came.

"I know you can hear me. I know you haven't left yet. It's okay if you don't want to talk to me. I understand. I am not really part of your life. In some strange way, I'm from your future — a possible future. Except that even that's not it really. But we are connected — we are blood.

"I don't know what to think of you. But if I'm going to die today, then you need to know a few things. Mostly, I forgive you. Not you, of course, but the other you — the one that lived on to become my mother. I forgive you for leaving me and leaving me so empty. I forgive you for hiding this world from me. I forgive you for everything.

"As kids we see our parents as figures — not quite human. But you are. You have your faults and your desires and you made so many mistakes. I spent too much time wishing things were different, wanting to find my lost time as if that might fill the lost things within me. But that's not true. Here I stand, with part of you filling me right now, yet I'm every bit as scared as I would've been without you. I'm every bit as empty.

"If I survive this, then you should know that I love you,

I forgive you, and I will figure out how to move on.

"My lost time — I'll still find it. But if a part of you could not fulfill me, then no memory will either. I'm going to find that lost time because Dad is still alive. He needs me. And I need to understand who he is.

"I'm going to find that lost time not to fill my past but to help forge my future."

Roni waited for the physical reaction from Maria but none came. That was okay. Saying those words, articulating those thoughts and feelings — that was what mattered.

"Besides, I give myself a twenty-percent chance of surviving this."

Part of her thought her odds were even worse.

The colors in the rift faded. Subtle at first, and Roni could not quite believe it. But Elliot had told her that would be the sign. That his power to amplify Maria's force would drain from the rift — and in that way, they would overload it. Simple enough.

Now for the hard part.

"Maria, please tell me, are you ready?"

Roni expected no answer, but the familiar warm flush invaded her skin. She started at the sensation, then settled into a comforting grin.

"Okay." She thought she should say more but the words did not come.

With a few awkward motions, she pulled her left arm free from the rock surrounding it like removing her arm from the sleeve of a heavy sweater. She then performed the same series of motions with her right arm. Against her belly, she brought her hands together.

Here we go. One... Two... Three...

Roni ripped the golem paper in two. And the rocks tumbled away. The weight lifted from her body and the rain-soaked air breezing in through the hole in the wall cooled her skin. She had to step over the small pile of rubble surrounding her but she managed.

As she approached the rift, as she felt its energy pulling from her even as Elliot pulled from it, the rifters seeped through the ceiling. They sensed her presence now.

"You're too late," she said, and without giving herself time to alter course, stepped into the rift.

CHAPTER 23

At the age of eleven, Roni and her friends found great amusement in going to the mall and walking up the down escalator at the correct pace so that they never changed position. Being inside the rift felt the same way. The rift tried to pull her down but Elliot's power kept her in the same spot. She felt motion yet remained motionless. And this struggle of energy thinned the rift walls so that she could see the rifters amassing in the basement.

A few of the daring purple-black smoke balls attempted to attack her. They barreled through only to be disintegrated the moment they touched her skin. She watched as the dark curls of smoke dissipated around her, and she wondered if it was her presence in the rift or that of Maria's which caused such destructive power. Another attacked her and died for the effort.

But this did not stop them. Like ants or locusts, these creatures understood the power that came from attrition. They continued to shove through the rift and slammed into her body. It did not hurt her, not much worse than a mosquito bite, but it most certainly killed them. Yet they continued to come.

Over time, like a water drip cutting through a stone, they would rip into her. The protection Elliot provided would not last forever. Neither would Maria. When those energies left, Roni knew what would happen to her — she had seen these creatures shred Sister Mary and Sister Claudia.

The air heated up around her, becoming like a bad sunburn. Still more rifters bulleted towards her. The bright orange air darkened with their purple corpses.

"Maria! Now!" The words scratched Roni's throat but she repeated them — louder each time.

All the noise and stress spun Roni's head in throbbing pain. She turned in a circle, and in every direction, she saw a greater number of rifters than before. They filled every location upon which her eye fell. They surrounded the rift and consumed all available space in the basement.

"Maria," she called again though slightly weaker.

When she thought to call out a third time, her feet lifted off the floor. The floor? Because she did not expect the floor within the rift. Because there wasn't one. The only floor around her was that of the church basement.

Roni watched as the basement ceiling came closer. She felt as if a coarse rope had been wrapped around her chest, lifting her up and forcing her arms out like wings. She was in the rift and the church simultaneously, fragmented between worlds, held in place by the same forces that threatened her.

Glancing down, the floor filled in beneath her with purple and black. It bubbled like a dark cauldron.

Please, Roni thought, *please Maria. Leave my body. Do what we came here to do.*

She would never understand why those thoughts worked when all her pleading and calling out had failed before. When she would think back upon this day, Roni always came to the same conclusion — that she had never understood Maria nor could she have. The trauma that girl had suffered, the oddities she had experienced, the frozen time and splitting from within herself — these were not experiences another human being could relate to. Whatever spurred Maria into action at that moment, Roni knew that she could never duplicate it.

Like tearing a hundred bandages off simultaneously, Maria stripped free. Roni shrieked. With both the speed of a bomb blast and the stillness of the rift's pulse, Roni experienced Maria's energy pouring out and amplified by Elliot.

A golden sunburst spread across the church. Wherever it touched a rifter, only wisps of gray smoke remained. Thousands of the creatures incinerated in seconds. Roni watched them slowly fall apart.

The distortion of time twisted her stomach even as it hypnotized her mind. The ceiling above her cracked apart, the wood floor of the nave giving way to the energy blast that had been Roni and Maria.

As time reconnected with itself to flow normally, Roni's body rose higher in the air. She slipped through the opening and lifted into the main part of the church.

The rifters soared away from her, the energy pulsing from her body repelling them. They pressed against the church walls like rats abandoning a sinking ship. But they could no longer slide through the stone. The walls glowed golden. They were stuck.

Roni's stomach clenched and her mouth opened. She expected to throw up but instead another blast of golden light erupted from her. It spread out in all directions, decimating the creatures that remained.

The sunburnt feeling on her skin worsened. She smelled burning flesh. Further in the distance, further than she could imagine, she heard a tinny voice. Almost like a coyote howling through a radio on a mountain miles away. But she heard it nonetheless. Calling her name.

... *roni* ...

The orange and red of the rift had gone. The purple and black had disappeared. All that remained was golden light.

And that distant voice. Calling her name.

... *roni* ...

A thin line of dark swiped across her field of vision. Again, she heard her name and again she saw the line. She tried to move her hand but it refused to obey her.

Roni felt as if she were once again surrounded by the stone golem — except this time it was golden light not gray rocks. This time, it was Maria. And the pressure upon her skin hurt. Burned.

Let go of me, she pleaded, but suspected Maria would never listen to her again.

Once more she heard that distant call and saw that gray line appear. This time she understood — *Gram.*

Thinking the name cleared her eyes. Roni saw Gram standing down on the nave floor, twirling a chain at her side. The walls of the church crumbled around her. Bits of stained-glass cracked and fell. Gram remained standing in place throwing her chain at Roni, all of her being focused on trying to lasso her granddaughter.

As the chain soared through the air once more, Roni watched it head directly for her. Except it diverted at the last moment as if it had been swatted aside by an invisible hand. It passed before her eyes like it had each time previously.

Gram gazed up at Roni, the desperation consumed the air between them. Roni tried to call out, try to tell Gram to give it another go. No words would leave her mouth.

Calling her name again, Gram twirled her chain once more. But she sounded so far away — *roni.*

Roni closed her eyes. She focused all of her mind and energy into her right arm. And she felt it — that sickly-sweet energy. Maria. The last vestiges of her existence, the part of her that had kept her alive all those years in the rift, the will that refused to end.

Maria did not mean to harm her — at least, Roni did not think so — but she also intended to keep Roni. Perhaps Maria did not want to let go of her connection to her past, even if that meant hurting Roni. Perhaps she only wanted to go on existing, no matter the consequences, no matter what the rest of her desired.

With every fiber of mental strength she possessed, Roni pushed Maria away and reached toward Gram. And she listened. And she waited.

When she heard Gram call her name once more — *roni* — she snapped her eyes open. The chain sailed towards her, and as it had each time before, it curved away. Except this time Roni thrust all of her thoughts into her right hand. The fingers flipped open and the rosary beads stretched out — far enough to make contact with the chain.

Gram paused, astonished at her success as the chain snapped onto the beads. But she was a professional of the Parallel Society. She wouldn't waste time. Within the next second, she pulled Roni as she backed up towards the exit.

Time threatened to rip apart again. Roni sensed it splitting down her mind. This would be the last time. If Maria held too tight, Roni did not think she would ever get free.

Please, Roni thought with all the firm compassion she could summon. *We love you. But it's time for you to leave. It's time for you to rest.*

Still, Maria held on.

Let me go! Let yourself go! You … you're not my mother. You're not even Gram's daughter. You need to find your own life, your own future, your own peace.

Words continued to tumble out of Roni like a riffing poet. She did not think her pleading would amount to anything, but then she felt a cold chill slip out of her spine. It did not hurt — it was like having an icy hand slowly remove itself.

And she was free.

Two arms, two thick arms Roni knew so well, wrapped around her. Gram kissed her face as she lugged Roni out of the church. Raindrops pelted them, and Roni's legs refused to help, but Gram kept dragging her to safety.

Sitting on the ground with her back against the rental car, Roni watched as Sully and Elliot and Gram eased next to her. Three loud cracks like dynamite signaled the end of the church. In a plume of stone and debris, the old building crumbled to the ground.

As the sound quieted and only the patter of rain remained, Sully returned to his feet and set his hands on his hips. "Well, this is going to take some explaining. Governments can be a real pain in the tush." He turned toward the group. "Is everyone okay?"

All eyes rested on Roni. She gazed back at them. "Me? I feel fine. Absolutely —"

Her head grew heavy and rolled toward the ground as her eyes closed.

CHAPTER 24

Despite her exhaustion, Roni knew sleep would not be coming anytime during the flight home. The boys had no trouble, though. Elliot's serene face across the aisle exuded peacefulness while Sully's deep snores could be heard from several rows back. Gram sat next to Roni, reading her Bible while taking surreptitious glances in Roni's direction.

For the first few hours, Roni buried her attentions in her journal. She detailed the events at the Abbey as best as memory served her, recording all the names, creatures, experiences, everything. She made sure to include that after the collapse of the church, Elliot spent over an hour casting for any sign of Maria, the creatures, or the rift itself. They were all gone. Maria had been set free, the creatures had all been consumed by the rift, and the rift — well, the rift had been closed. Not contained in a book, not stabilized in a state of half-existence, but actually closed. To the best of Roni's limited knowledge, no rift had ever been closed before.

She wrote on about her thoughts and feelings concerning the work they did and how close she had come to losing her life. Not only was it her duty as the researcher and librarian of the Parallel Society to record this information for future Society members to use, but she found it therapeutic. If she did not spew these thoughts onto the page now, she would spend many years ahead of her in expensive therapy.

Later, after a bland and overpriced sandwich, Roni shifted in her narrow seat to face Gram. They had spoken little about Maria since leaving the Abbey, and she had no intention of starting now. However, thinking through all that had transpired so she could write it down, several questions poked at her mind.

Gram leaned her head towards Roni. "Out with it. Whatever's got you thinking, you're going to burst if you don't ask."

With an embarrassed chuckle, Roni said, "I want to ask you about my dad. I've always thought he ended up in a mental hospital because of the car accident, because of losing her. But that isn't true, is it?"

"Oh, I don't know. Your father was always tight-lipped about the thoughts in his head. I do know that he lost touch with reality when your mother died. That was the timing of it, and that was the easiest answer for you to understand at such a young age."

"But he knew about the Parallel Society."

"No, he didn't." Gram spoke as if the very idea fouled the food in her stomach.

Roni wanted to argue, wanted to point out that she had spoken with him at length, and that he had indicated knowledge of the real world, of the Parallel Society, of everything. Perhaps Mom had told him. Perhaps he knew about Roni's past and therefore what the future held for her.

But she held back. Gram had not experienced the same things she had at the Abbey. While Roni had little problem letting go of the past and her lost time — at least, in terms of solving that mystery and filling the void — Gram would not see it the same way. To her, the past had been a secret she carefully guarded. Whether to protect Roni or to protect the Parallel Society or to protect herself, Roni did not know.

And, Roni thought, *she really does care.* The past was only important in how it affected the future. That was why she needed answers about her dad.

"I don't mean to speak ill," Gram said, "but have you ever considered the possibility that your father's mental illness does not come from any trauma caused by your mother, me, or any of this? Perhaps, his mental illness is no different than anybody else's. Perhaps his brain's wires simply are not functioning properly."

"I'll have to think about that." Roni said it to appease Gram, but neither of them appeared to believe the words much.

She returned to her journal, reading over all she had written in the last few months. Her father had warned her over a year ago that something dark and dangerous had begun. She did not give it too much credence back then, but after the Abbey, she wondered.

The rift had been stabilized for centuries, yet it suddenly changed its behavior. Of course, her mishandling of the situation and using the old book caused much of it — but what if there were other forces also at work?

When she got home, she would have to hit the books. Research was her skill for the Parallel Society and she needed to use it now more than ever. But that awaited her at home. And while she had made the choice not to dwell on her past, she saw no harm in spending a few moments basking in the warmth of her success.

They had saved the Earth from an invasion, released

Maria from her prison, and closed a rift. Not bad for a couple days work.

Roni's adventures continue in
LOST TIME

In her short time with the Parallel Society, Roni Rider has faced many deadly creatures and horrifying situations. But nothing haunts her more than her Lost Time -- the large gaps in her memory stolen when she was a child. For Roni, it is a constant reminder the she is incomplete.

When a creature from deep within the Caverns reaches out to her, she is set upon a journey that will take her beyond anyplace she could imagine, a journey to find out what was stolen and why. She'll discover the truth behind her missing past, the dark secrets that had been kept from her for years, and the horrible repercussions of it all.

But first, she'll have to remember how she got there.

The Max Porter Paranormal Mysteries!

When Max Porter discovers his office is haunted by the ghost of a 1940s detective, he does the only sensible thing - he starts a detective agency with the ghost!

Don't miss a single story in the bestselling series, the Max Porter Paranormal Mysteries.

ABOUT THE AUTHOR

Stuart Jaffe is the madman behind *The Max Porter Paranormal Mysteries,* the *Nathan K* thrillers, *The Parallel Society* series, *The Malja Chronicles, The Bluesman, Founders, Real Magic,* and so much more. His unique brand of old pulp adventure mixed with a contemporary sensibility brings out the best in a variety of SF/F sub-genres. He trained in martial arts for over a decade until a knee injury ended that practice. Now, he plays lead guitar in a local blues band, *The Bootleggers,* and enjoys life on a small farm in rural North Carolina. For those who continue to keep count, the animal list is as follows: one dog, two cats, two aquatic turtles, and fifteen chickens. The horse is now at a new pasture. She's having a wonderful time hanging with a herd of thirty other horses. Much better for her. As best as he's been able to manage, Stuart has made sure that the chickens do not live in the house.

Made in the USA
Coppell, TX
14 November 2021